JUST ASK
IRIS

ALSO BY THE AUTHOR

I Am an Artichoke

Will You Be My Brussels Sprout?

Oy, Joy!

JUST ASK
IRIS

BY LUCY FRANK

A RI
ATHEN   S
NEW YORK   E

I would like to thank Nelson Peña
for his help and encouragement throughout
the writing of this book.

Atheneum Books for Young Readers
An imprint of Simon & Schuster Children's Publishing Division
1230 Avenue of the Americas
New York, New York 10020

Book design by Michael Nelson
The text of this book is set in FilosofiaRegular.

Printed in the United States of America
2 4 6 8 10 9 7 5 3 1

Library of Congress Cataloging-in-Publication Data
Frank, Lucy.
Just ask Iris / by Lucy Frank.—1st ed.
p.   cm.
"A Richard Jackson book."
Summary: In the summer before seventh grade, twelve-year-old Iris
Diaz-Pinkowitz goes up and down the fire escape outside her new New York
City apartment, becoming an integral part of the lives of
her human and animal neighbors.
ISBN 0-689-84406-9
[1. Apartment houses—Fiction. 2. Neighbors—Fiction.
3. Resourcefullness—Fiction. 4. Cats—Fiction.
5. New York (N. Y.)—Fiction. 6. Humorous stories.]
I. Title.PZ7. F8515 Ju 2002
[Fic]—dc21   00-049592

FIRST
F
EDITION

For Peter, as always;
also for all my cats, past and present;
and for all my neighbors.

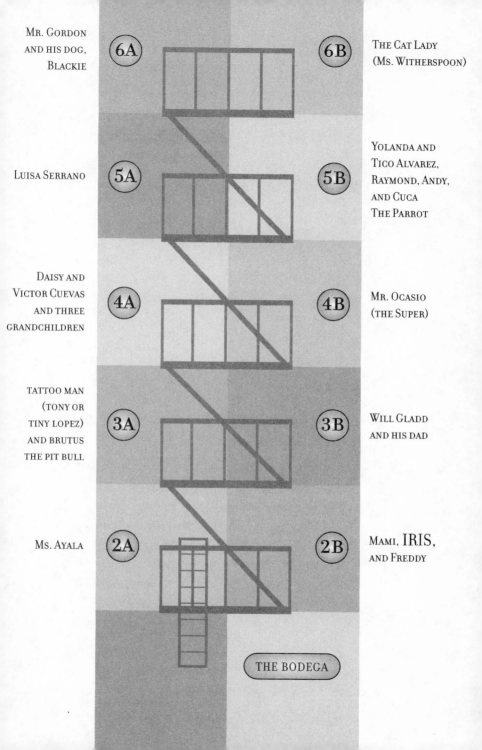

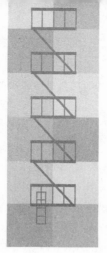

CHAPTER 1

"*AAAAAAAAH*, A RAT! OH MY GOD! *DIOS MÍO!*
There's a rat in the bed!"

I'd just fallen asleep when I heard Mami screaming. I jumped up, grabbed the staple gun and a paint
roller, and ran to her.

"Iris, stay back!" Freddy stood in the doorway to
the living room with his baseball bat. Mami was hopping around like the floor was on fire. "It's okay, Ma!
Calm down! Relax!" He rushed in and poked the
bat into the corners of the pullout sofa. "Which way'd
he go?"

"I don't know!" Mami climbed up on a chair. "All I
know, he was huge! He was making the whole bed
shake, he was so big."

Freddy stuck his bat under the sofa, peered under
the desk, moved the bookcase. "He's not here now. I'd

have seen him if he ran past. Ma, maybe you were dreaming."

"No!" she said. "That rat was sniffing and snuffing right next to me! Ay, *Dios!* I'm never going to get back to sleep until I know he's gone."

Mami is one of those people who, if she's awake, she has to be working at something, and if she's working, she thinks everyone else should be working, so we spent the next hour looking in all the closets and all the corners in every room, stuffing steel wool around the heat risers and nailing a board over the hole behind the sink. "And first thing tomorrow," she said, "we're setting traps. I don't care how much painting and fixing up we did this week. That rat goes or we move right back out of here."

"Back to the Bronx?" I said. "To Grandma's?" We'd moved around a lot—to nice places when Papi was working, not so nice when he wasn't—but never to one with rats. And, until eight days ago, never without Papi. "It's okay with me if we go back," I said.

"I know, *m'ija.*" A tired look came into Mami's eyes, but only for a second. "But that's not going to happen."

"Yeah." Freddy was still pumped. "I can just see Papi if a rat got in bed with him. He'd probably try to sell him a piece of cheese." He went into a phony chuckle. "Heyyyy there, Chief! How you doin', my friend? Can I interest you in a nice used chunk of cheddar? Have a seat. I'll be with you in a minute. Soon as this show's over."

He was working hard, trying to make Mami laugh. She always said how when Papi was flopped down in front of the TV you could yell, "Fire!" and Papi'd just say, "Oh yeah, what channel?" But she wasn't doing much laughing lately. Freddy'd started calling her The Vacuumator, because of this look she got—like the old Hoover was a power eraser and she was on an erasing mission from God. We'd been seeing that look a lot. And not just when she was vacuuming.

"Ma, d'you see Iris with that staple gun?" He was still trying. "Back off, sucker, or I'll staple your foot to the floor! You better watch out, or I'll paint you pink!"

"Hey, I was ready to defend us," I said. "I grabbed the first things I saw."

I wasn't feeling much like laughing, either. I didn't like it here even before the rat. It was a big apartment, and we'd gotten it amazingly clean, but the rooms, except for the bathroom, were in a line, so that you couldn't get from the front door to the kitchen without going through the bedrooms. My room was next to the kitchen, which was good if I got hungry in the middle of the night, but bad if someone else did. It was the beginning of August, and way too hot to sleep. I couldn't get used to the trucks roaring down the avenue, the

3

fire engines and car alarms, the people in the street talking and singing, breaking bottles, playing music till all hours. Plus, I missed Papi. Plus, if we went back—even if it hadn't been too great these past months with all of us living with his mother, everyone screaming and yelling all the time—I wouldn't have to go through the whole new school, new friends thing again.

But there's only so much feeling bad I can do, and only so much worrying, so when I got back in bed, I started reading *The Power of Sexual Surrender*. It was this old, musty, serious brown book with gold lettering, so I could tell when Mami came to kiss me good night, she thought it was like Shakespeare or something. But my face must have given me away, because she grabbed it from me.

"Uh-uh! No! Forget it!" she said. "You're not reading that! Where'd you get it from, your brother?"

"No," I said. "It's Grandma Lillian's. She even made stars by some of the things in it. Wanna see?"

Mami may have been laughing, but she was not giving that book to me. "No, I don't wanna see!" she said. "And neither do you. You're twelve years old, Iris. You're a kid. And as long as I've got anything to say about it, that's how you're staying."

The next morning I offered to go down and get the rat traps. Big excitement, right—a rat trap-buying

4

expedition. But we'd been here over a week, and Mami still hadn't let me go anywhere without her or Freddy. The bodega was just downstairs, so she couldn't say no. But I didn't even get to enjoy my freedom when these three jerks standing around outside started making kissing noises, saying stuff to me.

"*Psst! Mira, linda!*"

"*'Ey, Preciosa, ven aquí!*"

"Good morning, lovely. Want a little sip of my coffee? It's hot and sweet, just like you—"

Those twenty feet to the bodega felt like twenty miles.

The place was full of people buying milk or Pampers or lottery tickets or standing around drinking *café*, talking to the owner. He gave me a nice hello. I took as long as I could picking out the traps, hoping the guys would be gone when I came out, but no.

"What's your name, sweetheart?"

"C'mon, baby, don't be like that. Come over here and say hello."

"Yo, you're kinda young to have such an attitude—"

"And you're kinda old to be acting stupid!" I wish that had been me talking. It was a middle-aged lady wheeling a little boy in a grocery cart. A boy and a girl walked on each side. "Ralphie, does your wife know you're out here bothering people? *Y tú*, Flaco, what's your problem?" She scolded them in English, then in

5

Spanish. I caught some of it before I ducked into the building.

She came in after me. "Thank you, honey," she said as I held the door so she could get through with the grocery cart. "Don't worry. They won't be bothering you anymore. I know them since they were my grandkids' age. You're in 2B, right?" I nodded. "Yeah. I seen you moving in. This is Frankie, Jessica, and Joey." They were cute kids. She lifted the little boy out and stood him on the floor. We started up the stairs. I couldn't wait until they fixed the elevator. The hall smelled really bad, and the yellowish light on the pukey tan walls and dark brown banisters made me feel like we were in a dirty fish tank. "And I'm Daisy, 4A. What's your name?"

"Iris," I said.

"Pinkowitz?"

I nodded.

"Yeah, I seen your name on the mailbox and I said to myself, Pinkowitz? Isn't that a Jewish name? Because you don't look Jewish."

This happened basically every time I met people. Just, some people didn't come out and say it. That was the worst part of starting a new school, telling kids my name. You'd think teachers would be better. . . .

"And isn't your mother that pretty dark-skinned lady I saw on the stairs the other day? Latina, right?"

Even before she'd turned into The Vacuumator, Mami would have told Daisy to mind her business. She says she doesn't know where people get off thinking they can just come up to me and Freddy and ask us what we are. "People aren't happy until they know what box to put you in," she says. And yet Daisy had stuck up for me out on the street, so I said, "Yeah, that's my mother." But then I could feel her getting ready to say, "I haven't seen your father." So I hurried up the last few steps to my floor and took out my keys. "Thanks," I said.

She smiled. "No problem. A word to the wise, honey. Tell your mother to buy you a brassiere. You'll have a lot less trouble with these morons if you've got a bra."

What? Without even saying bye, I ran in, ran to the bathroom, and checked myself from the front, from the side, from the other side: a tall, tan-skinned kid, with long brown hair pulled tightly back, big eyes only a little darker than my skin, glasses, long, skinny legs, and—oh my God, I really did need a bra!

Why didn't I know this? I mean, I did know this, but I'd been telling myself no one else did.

Mami was in the kitchen ironing the white polo shirts she wears for work. "Mami," I said, "I need a bra!"

She put the iron down and took the traps from me. "Why you bringing that up right now? Iris"—she looked at me closely—"did something happen?"

If I told her about those guys, she'd be down the stairs so fast . . . and if I told her about Daisy . . . "No." I prayed my face wasn't as red as it felt. "I'm just asking."

"Well, ask me after I'm back at work, okay?" she said. "When things are more settled. When we've got some money. Iris, I've got so much on my mind now . . ."

Mami worked at Graciela's, a restaurant a few blocks from here. She'd taken two weeks off to get us moved. Her first day back was tomorrow. She wasn't worried about Freddy—Freddy was a boy and fourteen—but she was very nervous about leaving me. She'd already given me tomorrow's TO DO and NOT TO DO lists, and there were twice as many NOT TO DOs as DOs.

There was no point asking her anything when she was in that No mode. But the longer I waited, the bigger my—I didn't know what to call them even to myself. It wasn't them I minded. It was the words for them. "Puberty" was bad enough, with that *pyou*, like putrid or puke or mucus. I didn't need body parts with names that made boys snicker and whisper and poke each other and point and stare. Not now, when everything else in my life was changing. They looked like they'd grown just since this morning and, going by Mami's, they'd keep on growing. Which meant that by the time school started, in five weeks . . .

"Ma," I said after Freddy had gone into his room that night, "everyone I know has had bras since the middle of fifth grade."

She stopped dabbing peanut butter on the rat traps. "Yeah, and I bet some of them are having babies, too."

"What does that have to do with getting me a bra?" I said. "I thought this was about money."

"It is," she said. "But also, we're in a new situation. It's going to be much less stressful. The Computer School's supposed to be a really good place, and now that we've got Aunt Myra's computer, and that typing book—"

Grandma's typing book? "Mami, you keep changing the subject."

"I'm not changing the subject," she said. "It's the same subject. Freddy I've given up expecting A's from. But you're different, Iris. You're like me at your age. You're smart. You could do so well. . . ." She finished setting the traps, put one behind the fridge and another in the corner. "Iris, *mi amor*, you have the whole rest of your life to be grown up. Take it from me, there's nothin' that great about it. Don't rush it."

"I'm not rushing it," I said. "Ma, look at me."

She came over and kissed me. "I don't have to look at you. You look fine. You look like a beautiful young girl who's going to turn into a beautiful young lady. But for now, do us all a favor. Stay a kid."

Stay in the house was more like it. Put an overshirt over my undershirt and my shirt. And when school started, wear my backpack on my front, like this girl, Marisa, who all of a sudden wore like a 38D and had to keep her coat on, and wear her backpack right under her chin, and walk bent over like a hunchback so the nasty boys wouldn't be grabbing at her. It was hard enough that at every school I'd been to there were the Spanish kids, the black kids, a few Asian kids, a few white kids, and me and Freddy. Except when we were at Grandma's and there were the Italian kids, the Jewish kids, a couple Asian kids, and me and Freddy. I didn't know who'd be at this Computer School. I did know I could not deal with them staring at me, going, "Pinka-*who? Pinka-what's that? Excuse* me? I beg your pardon? Uh, what *are* you, anyway?" Plus gawking at my chest.

Mami was always saying how smart I was. So then how come, no matter what school I went to, as soon as I walked through the door my brain jumped ahead, or stayed behind, or froze up totally, so that my teachers were always like, "Iris, would you care to join us?" "Iris, what planet are you on?" "Hello, Iris, anybody home?" Except Ms. Ragusa, in the fourth grade, who loved me because she was so glad somebody wasn't acting up, she could care less if I was listening.

Mami had hidden *The Power of Sexual Surrender*, so when I got in bed I tried *Exodus*, which I'd also found on Grandma's shelf.

I'd only been asleep a little while when I felt something walking on my bed. "Mami! The rat!" I shrieked. "Freddy, get the bat!"

"Where? Where is it?" Freddy ran in. "I can't see a thing."

"It's right here!" I was too scared to move. "Why isn't it running away?"

Mami flipped on the light. "*Ay, Dios!* I don't believe it!"

"Oh my God!" I said. "Thank God it didn't step in the trap!" Because it wasn't a rat. It was a cat, a gigantic, longhaired orange cat with a big head, a puffy tail, and a hunk missing from one ear. He gave us a look like we'd just messed up his plans for a good night's sleep, and jumped down.

"Yo, that's some rat, Ma! No wonder the bed was shaking." Freddy crouched and held out his hand. "Here, kitty, kitty . . ."

The cat sat down and started cleaning his fur.

"He must have come down the fire escape," I said. The fire escape was outside our kitchen window, on the back of the building.

"Yeah, but how'd he fit through the gate?" Mami said. "He's bigger than our Thanksgiving turkey. Look at him! He's not moving. He's acting like he lives here."

"Maybe he used to!" I said. "Maybe he belonged to whoever lived here before. Maybe that's why he keeps coming back."

"Maybe he just likes us," Freddy said.

The cat looked up at me with his round yellow eyes. "He's lonely," I said. I went to pet him.

"Don't touch him!" Mami said. "He's all nasty. He could have fleas."

"Careful, Ma!" Freddy said. "You don't want to insult this cat."

The cat stood up and started toward the kitchen. We followed it. Mami waved her arms at him. "Shoo! Get outta here!"

"Don't put him out," I said. "Please! I like him. He's so cute."

But the cat jumped up on the windowsill and squeezed himself through the security gate and out onto the fire escape.

I'm gonna go up tomorrow and look for him, I almost blurted. But since DON'T GO UP FIRE ESCAPE was on Mami's NOT TO DO list, right after not talking to strangers, and never going farther than the corner except with Freddy, I decided to keep my mouth shut.

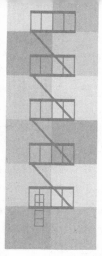

CHAPTER 2

PRACTICE TYPING
CLEAN MIRRORS
VACUUM KITCHEN
EMPTY WASTEBASKETS
WIPE OUT FRIDGE
MAKE CHOCOLATE PUDDING (IF YOU WANT)
START DINNER

I was looking at the TO DOs the next morning, wondering if Mami'd care if I made the pudding and ate it all right now, wondering what in the world I was going to do with myself after the chores were done, if there was anyone from the Bronx I could call, when I got that creepy back-of-the-neck feeling you get when someone's staring at you.

The cat was peering at me through the window gate.

"Hey!" I went over to the window. "I was gonna go look for you."

His mouth opened. *"Mewp!"* he said.

I mewped back at him.

"Mrrp," he said.

His eyes were big and round and almost the same tan-yellow as mine. His hair was fluffy and nice. When he wasn't mewping or mrrping, he looked like he was smiling. So he had no neck, and some scars on his nose, and that chewed-up ear. I didn't see why Mami thought he was nasty.

"You want to come in?" I said. "That's what you're saying? You're lonely?" I unlocked the gate, opened the window from the bottom, and in he hopped.

"I bet you're hungry, too." I got a slice of bologna from the fridge. He sniffed it. I dropped it on the floor. He didn't gobble it. He ate it neatly and then smiled up at me, so I gave him another, and then another. "You like it here with me, right?"

He sat down, cleaned his face with his paws, and started purring.

I'd never had a cat. Freddy had a turtle once, and I had two goldfish I won at a street fair until one time when Papi was drinking, he accidentally knocked the fishbowl down. I wondered if cats liked chocolate pudding.

I made it. He did.

"You gonna keep me company while I do my chores?" I said when he'd finished licking the bowl. I never knew cats could purr so loud.

He rubbed against me as I cleaned the bathroom mirror, then came in my room with me, and when I finished in there and opened Freddy's door, walked right through. That didn't worry me. Freddy could sleep through anything. It did worry me when we got to the living room and he jumped up on the computer desk, walked across it, and plopped himself down on the sofa. Except he looked so comfortable. And I did love to hear him purring.

I was checking my chest as I polished Mami's mirror, wondering if I should look in her dresser for some bra I could use without her missing it, when the phone rang.

It'd have been great if it was one of my friends from the Bronx, but it was Mami. "How're things going?" she said.

"Fine. Just a second." I leaned over and pushed the cat off the sofa. He jumped up on the desk, stepped over the keyboard, lay down in front of me, and rested his chin on my arm.

"So what are you doing?" Mami asked.

PRACTICE TYPING was the first thing on her list. "Getting ready to type," I said, praying she couldn't hear him purring. "I just finished spraying all the mirrors. And making pudding."

"And you're not too lonely?"

"No." I stroked his back. "I'm fine."

"How's the book look to you?"

"It looks fine." If I moved his tail, I could see it perfectly: *The Famous Dornbush Typing Method. Let Dr. Mildred Dornbush Help You Avoid Common Typing Pitfalls.* So I hadn't lied.

When I got off the phone, I opened the typing book.

ARE YOU GUILTY OF THE SLOPPY HABIT OF STRIKEOVERS?

I checked another page.

Type each line five times. DO NOT PEEK at the page. NEVER strike carelessly without thinking. THINK before you type.

A lad has a glad dad; dad had half a shad salad.

A hag has a lash as a fad.

Ask a lass a gag.

See how much you have accomplished in your first hour of instruction!

Now type each line five more times.

And another.

Good posture is vital to good typing.
Good posture is vital to good typing.
Good posture is vital to good typing.

Practice and determination are further aids.
Practice and determination are further aids.
Practice and determination are further aids.

"I'm determined," I told the cat. "Determined not to do this."

"Yo, Iris, who you talking to?" Freddy came in, rubbing his eyes. Then he saw the cat stretched out on the desk. "Whoa! Ma's going to kill you!"

"No, she won't," I said. "You're not going to tell her."

Wait a minute. Was that the cat he was staring at, or was it my chest? Maybe I should have taken a bra from Mami's dresser. Mami was kind of plump, though, and I might be getting big, but . . . "Freddy?" I said. "You got any money I can borrow?"

"For what, cat food?" He went over and scratched the cat behind the ears, then smelled his hand.

"He doesn't stink," I said. "He's very clean. No, not cat food. Just something I need to get."

"How much are we talking?"

How much did bras cost? "I don't know, twenty?" Freddy had money. Freddy was supposed to look out for me and take me anywhere I needed to go. There had to be stores in the neighborhood that sold them.

"Twenty bucks?" He shook his head. "I could give you three, maybe—"

"Never mind." I'd have been way too embarrassed to tell him what I wanted it for, anyway.

Freddy went out, but the cat stayed with me all morning. After he climbed back out the window, I wiped the bologna grease off the kitchen floor, vacuumed, and made sure to close the bottom of the window so he wouldn't come in while Mami was there.

"The house looks so nice!" Mami said when she got home. "What'd you do, vacuum the whole place?"

I nodded.

"How'd you do with the computer?"

"Not bad," I said. Which still wasn't a lie, since it couldn't be bad if I didn't do it.

The next morning, the cat was back mewping outside the window. "Hello, Mewper," I said as I opened the window for him. He went right to the refrigerator, so I gave him some leftover chicken. He liked that even better than bologna. The next day, I gave him rice and beans. He loved the rice and beans.

It was like he wore a watch. Every day at five of nine, there he was, looking for his breakfast. We'd do whatever was on Mami's list, which never took long—typing was at the top of every list, but I skipped it—then I'd get something for him and something for me, and go out on the fire escape and eat with him.

The fire escape looked out over the courtyard, and when there was any breeze at all, it was a lot cooler than inside. If I leaned over the railing, I could almost touch the tree growing out of the cement. I liked this tree, even if it did have a pair of pajama bottoms caught in the branches. I liked how its shiny, reddish leaves shivered in the breeze and how the breeze made the pajama bottoms seem to dance. It was so peaceful being out here with him. He'd eat his Rice Krispies and then, at lunchtime, his rice and beans or whatever, and sit there with me in the sun, his paw draped over my arm, and purr. Sometimes I read, but sometimes I just sat and listened to him. Something about that purr made me forget all my worries. I thought a few times about trying one of Mami's bras so I could go out, only with him around, I didn't mind staying in.

But I could never get him to stay all day. If I went inside to the bathroom, or to get the phone, he'd leave. I looked up and down the fire escape, but I never saw him.

"I wish I knew where he lived," I told Freddy.

"He's an alley cat," Freddy said. "He jumps onto that Dumpster in the courtyard, right? Then he climbs up the side of the building to the ladder"—he pointed to the ladder on the fire escape, which hung down from the third floor to just below our floor—"and he's here. Or he could be a roof cat, or a bodega cat. I've seen cats down there."

Wherever he came from, I was starting to think of him as my cat. I'd even given him a name: Fluffy.

"I'd have said Scruffy," Freddy said. "Or Tuffy. Or Tubby."

"No, he's a great cat," I said. "Right, Fluffernut? Mr. Comfort Cat?" I hugged him.

Freddy stuck his finger down his throat and made gagging noises. But I'd seen him bouncing his yo-yo for Fluffy to bat at.

Fluffy came every day that week. But Saturday there was no sign of him. Mami was working. She'd arranged with Graciela to work every day for the month between now and Labor Day to make up for the time she'd taken off when we were moving. I went out on the fire escape a million times looking for him. I called. I left a chicken wing under the window ledge, where Mami wouldn't see it. It was still there Sunday afternoon.

So, even though it felt like a thousand degrees out, I put on long pants, buttoned up my overshirt, and went down to the bodega. Fortunately, there were no jerks out today. It was probably too hot for them. I was also relieved not to see Daisy.

"I'm trying to find a cat," I told the owner.

"We got cats. How many you want?" He pointed behind some cases of toilet paper at two cats the same orange color as Fluffy.

"Those are your only ones?" I asked.

"Yeah, but I'll give you a good deal on 'em." He winked at the young guy behind the deli counter. "Two for the price of one."

"No thanks," I said.

"I'd be thanking you," he said. "Only reason I have 'em is to catch mice, *pero* these guys here haven't caught mouse one. I can't be feeding 'em two cans a day of Nine Lives if they don't earn their keep. I'll toss in a bag of litter just to get rid of 'em."

"That's okay," I said.

He looked me over. "You live upstairs, right? You're new."

"Yeah," I said, wondering if I had to go through a repeat of the whole Daisy thing. But he stuck out his hand, so I shook it and said, "I'm Iris."

"I'm Sammy." He smiled. "Welcome."

I explained to him about Fluffy.

"Ohh, that cat! Yeah, I know that cat. He's a monster. Right, Junior?" The young guy nodded. "*Como así*, right?" Sammy spread his hands three feet apart. "Yeah, he came in here one time, trying to beat up these guys. I had to chase him out with a broom." He laughed.

"You know where he lives?" I said. "Or where he went?"

"No, but he could be one of the Cat Lady's cats."

"The Cat Lady?" I asked.

"La morena vieja," said Junior. "You haven't seen her? The old crazy black lady in 6B? Cats and hats, that's her—"

"Yeah, she comes down here to buy her cat food in her hat and white gloves, like she's going to church," Sammy said. "I used to think she ate the stuff herself. Some people, you know, it's all they can afford to eat. Then Junior started delivering stuff up to her and—"

"And there were, like, cats everywhere, and she'd be like"—Junior went into a high, wobbly voice—"'Here you go, young man. This is for your trouble,' and she'd, like, hand me a quarter."

"Maybe I could go ring her bell and ask," I said, even though I hated the idea of taking those dark, smelly stairs all the way to 6.

"I don't know if I'd do that." Sammy tapped his forehead. "How many cats she has, Junior, thirty, forty?"

"A hundred?" Junior said.

"Maybe she just likes cats," I said.

"It's way beyond that," Sammy said. "It's a sickness. I don't know if she's, like, loony tunes, *pero* she ain't normal, that's for sure—right, Junior?"

"Yeah, you should see that place!" Junior laughed.

22

"And the smell! Whew!" He fanned the air. "It's sicken-ing."

"It's sad is what it is." Sammy shook his head. "It's pathetic."

"But you think this cat could be up there?" I asked.

"Anything could be up there," Junior said.

"Except for rats!" Sammy said. "No rats or mice in her house. *Mira*, if it was me, I'd find myself another cat."

It wasn't about another cat.

This lady did sound scary, though. Maybe even scarier than the stairs.

I went home to see if maybe Freddy'd go up with me, but Freddy had gone out. It was hours till Mami came home, with nothing to do but wonder about Fluffy, or read, which I was way too antsy for, or type— no, forget that—or sit around and watch my chest grow. Which brought back an idea.

In Mami's underwear drawer I found a thick, gray sports bra I was pretty sure she never wore. It almost fit okay after I pinned the straps and the back with safety pins. A little lumpy when I put my T-shirt on, but way better than no bra. Good enough so even without the overshirt, I wouldn't be embarrassed if I saw Daisy. And I really did miss Fluffy.

I didn't know yet if I would talk to the Cat Lady or just scope things out. But I went up the fire escape.

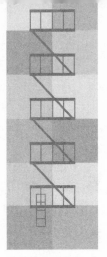

CHAPTER 3

"SHHH! NICE PIT BULL. GOOD DOGGIE."

The fire escape stairs went from right outside our window—the B apartment—to the A apartment. I was at the second-to-the-last step, just high enough to get a good look in 3A's window, when I saw this pit bull looking back at me.

"It's okay." I tried to sound calm and soothing. "I'm not gonna bother you."

He wasn't barking, just sort of grrrring quietly. I went up another step. The grrrrs got louder. The window was closed, so he couldn't have eaten me even if he wanted. I stepped onto the landing. There was no shade or curtains or security gate, so I could see the whole kitchen. Whoever lived in here had pizza and beer last night, ate Sugar Pops, and took a lot of vitamins. And had this really ugly dog.

Uh-oh. He was barking now.

Fire escapes have a wide part—maybe three feet wide and four feet long—right outside everybody's window, but between the two apartments, which is like ten feet, the platform narrows. I wasn't too crazy about walking across, even with the railing, but it was that, give up and go home, or stand here while this dog looked for a way to rip my throat out.

"Brutus!" called a rough, growly voice. "You yappin' at the pigeons again?"

I edged onto the narrow part, where I couldn't be seen, squashed myself against the side of the building, and peeked in.

The guy coming into the kitchen was like the person version of the dog—big and thick, with huge, bulging muscles, a shaved head, a silver ring in each ear, a stud in his nose and another in the middle of his chin, and a big blue spiderweb with a red spider tattooed on his elbow. He went to the counter, fished a slice of pizza from the box, gave half to the dog, and ate the other half. He was close enough now that I could see a tattoo on his other arm. It said either TINY or TONY. The writing was too hard to read. . . . Oh, no!

My flip-flop had come off. I bent over to get it.

"Yo, yo, kid! Whatchu doin' out there?" He came over to the window and, grabbing the dog by the collar, pushed the window wide open and stuck his face at me. "Yo, this ain't a peep show! It's my home."

His eyes were like Dracula's. I couldn't move. I couldn't swallow. "Sorry," I squeaked. "I'm really sorry. I didn't mean to peep." I could see his hands now. He had, like, vines tattooed on each finger.

"Whatchu looking at?" he growled.

"Nothing!" I said. "I'm just . . . looking for a cat. You didn't happen to see a big orange cat out here?"

"Let's see"—he stroked his chin—"has Brutus eaten any cats this week? Nah." He shook his head. "Not this week. Good thing I'm holding on to him, though, 'cause he also eats nosy *piojitas* who peep in his window."

It was all I could do not to race down the fire escape and jump headfirst into my apartment.

"This cat I'm looking for," I said instead, "I heard there's this person called the Cat Lady—"

"Yeah, and somebody ought to call the guys with the nets for her and her cats," he said. "Or I should send Brutus up there. He'd take care of 'em. No problem."

"So . . . that's where I was going," I said. "Up there. To 6B. If it's okay with you."

"I don't care what you do," he said. "Long as you stay away from my window."

So now I had no choice. I had to go on.

Slowly, carefully, making sure not to look down, I stepped across the platform to 3B, which was right above our apartment. The shade was pulled down. The window was open from the bottom about a foot. I had no idea who lived here. I prayed there were no dogs or Tattoo Men. But just as I was thanking God for letting me make it to the stairs alive, something got me on the leg. First I thought it was a bee. But it felt more like I'd been shot with something. It didn't draw blood, but it sure stung.

Mami was right. I should never go up the fire escape.

I did, though. And now 4A was Daisy. Even with Mami's bra on, I did not want to see Daisy. I made sure she wasn't in the kitchen before I stepped onto the landing. Her kitchen was as neat as ours. There was a high chair in the corner and a ride-on toy parked over by the door. I could smell beans cooking, and *pernil*. That roasting pork smelled delicious. If I was Fluffy, this was where I'd be. But I didn't see him, and I could hear the TV somewhere back in the apartment, so I went on across the platform. I was getting a little more used to the narrow part now. If you didn't look down, it wasn't really that scary.

Apartment 4B was the super's, Mr. Ocasio's. He was sitting at the table watching the ball game, reading the paper, and drinking a beer.

He looked up and saw me. "Hey! You're not supposed to be on the fyescate!" he shouted. "You could fall and break your neck!"

Mami would be upset if I pissed him off before he fixed the leak under our sink. "Sorry," I said. "It's just

for a minute. I'm being careful. I'm looking for a cat."
I described Fluffy. "Sammy in the bodega said he might
belong to the Cat Lady—"

"Don't talk to me about that lady! That lady is a pain
in my . . . she's gonna cost me my job. . . ." He stopped
looking at the TV. "You're not going up there, are you?"

"Uh, I was—"

"You do," he warned, "you'll be sorry. In fact,
go home right now. Otherwise, next time I see your
mother—"

"*Oye!* Hello? Excuse me." Daisy was leaning out
her window. "I know that cat you're talking about.
That big, fuzzy orange guy, right?" She motioned me
to come over.

Man, was I glad I had the bra, because the first
thing she looked at when I got there was my chest.

"You want to know something in this building,
chica, ask me," she said. "Don't ask Ocasio. He's too
much of a grouch." I looked over toward his window.
"It's okay. I say that to his face. Yeah, I see that cat all
the time, going up and down."

"You think he's the Cat Lady's?" I said.

"That I can't say," she said. "But I used to see her,
before the elevator broke, pulling her cats down the
street in one of them little red wagons. You know, the
kind kids used to have? She'd pull them to Broadway, a
whole bunch of them, talking to them every step of the

way, and them cats would just sit there. They wouldn't jump off or nothing. What kind of person does that? There's something off there. Ocasio's right. Stay away from the Cat Lady."

A yell came from somewhere in the apartment.

"'*Pérate!* Just a minute *papi!*" Daisy called. "By the way, I saw your mother on the street yesterday. I've seen her a few times. She's so pretty. She fixes herself up nice, too, but she has such a sad look on her face. I tried saying hello to her, but I can see she don't really want to be bothered, so I don't push it. You should tell her I sell Avon, though, so if she needs beauty products . . ." She gave my chest a last glance. "And tell her I'm glad to see she took my advice about the bra."

I stayed on Daisy's landing after she went in, trying to figure out which was worse, going back or keeping going. Everyone was saying stay away from the Cat Lady. But I'd come this far. And if I just took a quick peek in her window . . .

What decided me was the garden. The whole fifth-floor fire escape, narrow part and all, was full of roses and daisies and other plants I didn't know, and there were vines covered with beautiful blue flowers all across the railing. Mean people could not have flowers like that. Plus, halfway up the stairs to 6 sat two pretty cats.

I went back across toward Mr. Ocasio's window, and, when I was sure his attention was on the TV, dashed up the stairs. The big white cat watched me nervously, but the little gray one seemed like it was thinking about coming down to say hello.

I didn't see anyone in 5A's kitchen. "Hey, cat," I called. The little cat rubbed itself against the railing. I stepped onto the landing, trying not to knock over the Café Bustelo cans with flowers growing in them. This looked like an old person's apartment. There were pom-poms on the curtains and pill bottles on the table, religious pictures on the wall, and a plastic tablecloth meant to look like white lace. I moved onto the narrow part, stepping carefully around the tray of lettuce plants and the pepper plant with its tiny green peppers, and the three big tomato plants loaded with little red tomatoes.

Those tomatoes looked so delicious. I peeked into 5B. Good, no one there, either. At least I didn't think so. There was no gate or curtains, but a giant hanging plant blocked my view. I took a tomato. It *was* really good. It was the best tomato I'd ever had. Nobody could notice if I took another. I checked the window again, then ate a few more, then a few more, then a few more.

I was standing there, trying to work up my courage to go up the last flight—the flight that would lead me to the Cat Lady's—when a siren went off. It sounded like a car alarm, or an ambulance, but it was coming from right inside 5B's window!

Next thing I knew, somebody was screaming, "Help, call the police! *Policía!* Call the police!" in this rusty, squawky voice like a crazy person.

I scrambled back across the platform. The shrieks followed me. "Help! Police!" in Spanish and in English—so loud, it was a miracle I didn't knock down any flower-pots.

As I got to the stairs, a tiny old lady stuck her head out the 5A window. I stuffed the tomatoes in my pocket, not sure if I should keep running down the steps—to Mr. Ocasio's—or stop. The lady didn't look mad, just shocked. "What's going on?" she said in Spanish. My Spanish is pretty good from the summers I spent with my aunt and uncle in Puerto Rico. "Who are you?" The alarm was still going. "*Rrrrrrrrrrrr! Eeeeeeeeeee! Dingggg!*"

"Cuca, *cállate!*" the woman shouted. "What were you doing, eating his tomatoes?"

"I'm sorry!" Mami would go berserk if she found out.

"*Cálmate, nena.* It's okay. I've got plenty." She had friendly, bright eyes and even more wrinkles than Grandma Lillian. "But Yolanda's crazy parrot thinks they're all for him. He even goes off if the cats try to come onto his *fyescate.*"

"That's a bird?" My knees practically collapsed from relief.

She nodded. "That's Cuca."

"*Brrrrk!* Pretty Cuca! Squeezably soft! Yours for just nineteen ninety-five!"

I would have laughed then, except Mr. Ocasio stuck his head out his window. "Luisa," he hollered. "What's going on up there?"

"Just some little girl eating Cuca's tomatoes," the lady called back. "Don't worry, *Héctor, ella es una muchacha bien* nice."

"I told her to go home!" He climbed out onto the fire escape. "Go home now! *Y no suba mas pa ya arriba!*"

"*Awwwwk!* Blow your nose! Tie your shoes! Go home!" screamed Cuca.

I was afraid to go down with Mr. Ocasio standing there all red in the face, pointing his finger at me.

"It's okay, *nena.*" Luisa patted my arm. "Hector, go back inside. You'll miss your game. You'll give yourself a heart attack."

"Thank you!" I told her. "Thank you so much!"

The instant Mr. Ocasio went in, I ran down the stairs, raced past his window, across the narrow part to Daisy's window, and down the steps. But just as I reached the third floor, I got shot on the leg again.

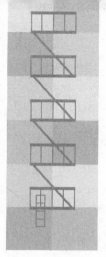

CHAPTER 4

"OW!" I SHOUTED.

Someone laughed. And I got shot again.

"Hey!" I crouched to look under the shade, but before I could see in, whoever it was pulled the shade the rest of the way down.

What, you haven't had enough scares for one day? Somebody shoots you and you're gonna stick your face in their window? I could hear Mami's voice in my head, loud as life, yelling at me to get out of here, get past Tattoo Man and his ugly dog, get home, and stay home.

But it was a kid's laugh. I was almost sure of it, and all the scared seemed to have been scared out of me, so I reached my hand in the window, grabbed the little ring on the bottom of the window shade, yanked, and let go. It rolled up with a loud snap.

A boy with a peashooter in his hand backed his wheelchair away from the window.

"What's wrong with you?" I yelled. "You just shot me!"

"Yeah, so?" he said with one of those looks teachers are always threatening to wipe off kids' faces. He looked older than me, but not a lot. His stringy brown hair hung down in his eyes. Without the smirk and that pale, pasty, pinchy look he'd have been cute. The top part of him seemed like a normal kid. He was too close for me to see his legs. I wondered what was the matter with him.

"What are you staring at?" he said.

I stopped staring, but I wasn't about to apologize. My leg still stung. "You, you jerk! You hurt me."

"Oodgie-boo-boo."

"What?" I hated this kid!

"What're you shouting for? It's just a pea."

"Excuse me. Three peas. What do you do, sit there looking for things to shoot?"

"Yeah. Pretty much."

"Well, cut it out."

"Well, what do you keep walking by for?"

"It's a free country," I said.

"My point exactly," he said.

"And I don't keep walking by. I walked by once."

I straightened up so I could see into the kitchen behind him. It was nasty in there—a mop sitting in the sink, a pile of old newspapers on the floor, a rickety table with a ketchup bottle, a bag of Wonder Bread, and a couple of cereal boxes on it. Then I saw the plastic bowl on the floor in the corner. My mind started racing. "Do you have a cat?" I said. Maybe Fluffy wasn't the Cat Lady's. Maybe he lived here.

"No, why?" He didn't look at me.

"'Cause there's a cat bowl over there." This was right upstairs from us. I could see why Fluffy didn't want to stay here.

"It's a dog bowl," he said.

"You have a dog?"

"I used to."

"So you don't have any pets now?"

"Nosy, aren't you?" he said.

"I was just wondering," I said.

"Yeah, well," he said, "my dad had him killed."

My stomach dropped. "Sorry."

His face didn't change. "You see those pigeons out there?" He nodded at the building across the courtyard. "How many do you think there are?"

"I don't know." I was still thinking about his dad and his dead dog, wondering again what was wrong with him.

"Just guess. How many? Take a guess."

I looked at the row of pigeons on the edge of the roof. "Twenty?"

"Try thirty-eight," he said. "Last week there were forty. The week before, there were forty-three."

"You shot them?"

He had that smirky smile again. "That's right."

"You killed five pigeons? With a peashooter?" I couldn't tell if he was lying. I didn't especially like pigeons, but I prayed he was.

"Yeah, with nails in it."

I jumped up. "What're you, crazy?"

"Where you going?"

"Where do you think? Away from you!"

"Good. You're not allowed to be out here, anyway. It's trespassing. It's a violation."

"The violation is to shoot at people," I said. "And that includes peas. I can be out here if I want. So forget about shooting me. You got that? You're not shooting me!"

"You won't be back here, anyway," he said. "Not if Brutus has anything to say. 'Shhh! Nice pit bull.'" He imitated me perfectly. "'Good doggie. Please don't eat me.'"

"I didn't say that."

"Yeah, you did."

So he'd overheard the whole Tattoo Man thing, including stuff I didn't even know I'd said out loud. I turned my back before I started across to 3A so he'd know I wasn't scared. I was pretty sure he wasn't going to shoot me again. But as I walked across the platform, praying that Brutus and Tattoo Man were asleep, or dead, or out taking a walk, I had a sickening thought: If Fluffy wasn't his cat, maybe this kid had shot Fluffy.

Fluffy would hardly feel a pea through his long fur. But a nail could kill him. Or hurt him really badly. He could be stuck on the roof or down in the courtyard with nobody to take care of him. He could be dying. I had to find him. How, though? And when? Mami would be home soon.

I made it past Tattoo Man's window without getting yelled or growled at and when I got back inside, I took off her bra and put it back in her drawer.

Mami came in so cheerful and chatty she didn't notice how shook up I was. "So I was talking to this lady who's a secretary," she said. "Telling her how you're going to this special magnet school. She was so excited you're learning typing. How's it going?"

"It's going." The last thing I could think about now was typing. "You know, Ma," I said, "I'm not going to The Typewriter School. It's The Computer School. This book was written before there even were computers."

"So you're doing it every day?"

"Pretty much." He could have shot and missed. Just scared Fluffy so that he didn't want to come back down the stairs. But I didn't know that. I didn't know anything. And now I couldn't go up to look until tomorrow.

"So then you must be starting to get good," Mami said.

"Pretty good." I didn't dare go up too early. I had to wait for Mr. Ocasio and Tattoo Man to go to work. Oh, God, please let Tattoo Man have a job! Please let me get past Cuca.

"Like how many words per minute?"

Out of the corner of my eye I could see she'd stopped chopping up the celery for our tuna salad. "I'm not sure."

"Let's see. Let's do a practice test. Just for fun."

I could feel the lie still on my face. "How 'bout a little later?"

"Why not now? It only takes a few minutes."

My blood drained to my feet as she came over to the table.

"Iris," she said, "I don't like the look on your face."

"What look?" I straightened the forks. Again.

"That look like you're lying to me."

My brain was blurring up the exact way it did at school. But I hated to disappoint her. Not to mention make her mad. "I'm not lying."

"I hope not," she said. "Because this is important. It's only four weeks till school." I tried to tune her words out by thinking about tomorrow, but it didn't work. "I don't get it. You're so smart, Iris. You do so well on those City and State tests. Even on the math ones you're, like, way up there. So then why, when there's something that's going to help you get ahead, do you have so much trouble focusing . . ."

They sent a letter home last year saying I had attention deficit disorder. Grandma thought it should be Papi who went in, because they'd listen more to someone white, but Mami put on her navy blue dress and her pearls and went roaring in with me to see the counselor. "She's reading four, five books a week," she said, "and I'm not talking easy readers. She can pay attention to everything but school. Which tells me you're the ones doing something wrong. Not her. Your school's the one with the disorder." It would have been embarrassing how loud she got if I wasn't so happy to have her sticking up for me. Of course, she gave me hell when we got home.

Which is not what I wanted now. "I'll type," I promised. "I'm focused. I focus really well. On lots of things. Just not school."

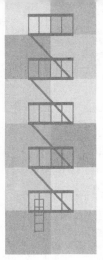

CHAPTER 5

THE NEXT MORNING, WHILE MAMI FOLDED UP the sofa bed, I read the book cover to her in my best Dr. Mildred Dornbush voice. "*The Famous Dornbush Typing Method*, by Dr. Mildred Dornbush, Professor of Education. 'Do you need help overcoming your fear of typing tests? Do you need to learn how to type in a hurry? This book has taught literally millions to type and it will teach you.'"

I'd hoped she'd laugh, but she said, "Okay. That sounds okay."

I made my voice even sterner and more booming. "'Lesson one. Keep your feet flat on the floor. Place your hands in your lap. Then, ra-a-a-a-aise them slowly so that the backs of your fingertips graze the front of the type- writer.' See, Ma, this book is, like, from nineteen fifty."

I had to look in the Cat Lady's window. If Fluffy was in there, I could stop worrying. If he wasn't, I'd have to think of something else.

"It doesn't matter. It's what Aunt Myra learned from. And it was a lot cheaper than buying a typing program." She looked up from straightening the cushions. "You don't have to do it all day. Just for an hour or so. An hour a day for the next four weeks and I promise, you'll be as good as anyone." She gave the pillows a last plump, then came over and kissed me. "Do it, Iris. I'll call in a little while to see how it's going."

It was too early to risk walking past Tattoo Man's window, anyway.

I'd worked on computers at school. I'd used the computers in the library. I'd played games on my friends' computers. This one was from Aunt Myra's job, and so old, we were lucky it had a mouse. It had no games. No Internet. Nothing fun. Just Microsoft Office. I opened a New Document the way Aunt Myra had showed me. I kept my feet flat on the floor. I placed my hands in my lap.

I'd do this till eighty-thirty or so, go up the fire escape, sneak across the platform, pull up the shade before the kid could get his peashooter, and say straight out, did you shoot Fluffy? I'd see what he answered. And take it from there.

Avoid the temptation to place your fingers on the home keys by sight. DO NOT LOOK AT THE KEYS.

It was too hot in here. I got up and turned on the fan. I got myself a drink. I listened to the Alleluya Man down below on the street, an old guy in a black suit who walked up and down carrying a Bible, chanting, "*Ahhhh-leluya, alleluya, alleluya, alleluya . . .*"

Let your fingertips creep lightly over the base until they barely touch the space bar.
Let your fingers bounce with each stroke.

There was a picture of a dorky lady with her feet flat on the floor and her fingertips creeping and bouncing. If that was Mildred, I felt sorry for her.

Asdfg space asdfg space asdfg space

Say the letters out loud as you type.
Do not forget to say the space.
Now type it again across four more lines.
DO NOT SKIP AHEAD!

I skipped ahead.

Now, without looking, say this combination until you can rattle it off from memory. DO NOT GO ON UNTIL YOU KNOW IT THOROUGHLY!

I turned the page.

Here we scramble the letters. YOU MAY NOT READ AHEAD! Keep your eyes on the copy and follow the dictation exactly. KEEP YOUR FINGERS ON THE KEYS!

Why did teachers always think they had to talk to you like you were a bad girl? A stupid bad girl. Or a bad dog. I was starting to hate Mildred. I was also starting to worry about seeing Brutus.

The buzzer rang. It was Kevin and Anthony, Freddy's friends from the Bronx. Saving me from Mildred! "Come on up," I said into the intercom. "I'll wake him."

"Freddy! Your friends are here!" I knocked on his door. Before I could put on Mami's bra and grab my overshirt, they rang the bell. I let them in.

"Yo, Pinky!" Anthony called. "Rise and shine, man. Up and at 'em!" He gave me a nod. "Whassup, Iris?"

"Yeah, whassup?" said Kevin, looking around the apartment. "Where's the Pinkster?"

"Right in there." I nodded toward his room then sat back down at the computer. Anthony had shaved his head since the last time I'd seen him. Kevin was trying to grow a goatee. Probably now Freddy'd be wanting a bald head, wishing he could grow a beard. Freddy always liked hanging out with older guys. He couldn't stand when they all called him Pinky but it had to be better than Shorty, which is what they used to call him.

"Yo, Iris"—Kevin came up behind me—"what ya' doin'?"

I pointed to the book. "I'm supposed to be learning how to type."

"Then how come there's nothin' on the screen?"

Anthony came over next to him, leaning closer so he could read over my shoulder: "'a lad has a glad dad; dad had half a shad salad.' Huh? Why'd he only have half? Who had the other half?"

"The lad." I looked up at him. He looked kind of cool with no hair. I smiled at him.

He laughed. "What *is* a shad?"

"It's a fish, stupid." Kevin was talking to Anthony but smiling at me.

"I knew that!" Anthony was smiling, too. "Iris, why you writing about fish? What is this?"

"It's Dr. Mildred Dornbush," I said. "She's taught millions to type and she can teach you."

"Look at this." Kevin leaned closer. "'dad has a gag; a lass has a sash; a lad had a lash as a fad.' This is stupid."

I usually thought guys looked dumb with earrings, but I liked his. "Yeah, it should say 'a lass's ass sat on her glasses.'"

"You just thought that up?" They both looked impressed.

I nodded.

"That's pretty good."

"It's easy," I said. "A lass has a glass ass. Hash gags a lad's dad. A lass has gas." I could have come up with even more, but Freddy was calling them. They looked at each other and went into his room.

"Yo, what were you doing in there?" I heard Freddy say before they closed his door.

"Talkin' to your sister!" Something about the way Anthony said it, I stopped trying to think up more sentences and went over to the door. "She's . . ."

I waited for him to say funny, or smart, maybe even pretty. But they both started laughing.

"She's hot, yo!"

They were both snickering. I froze.

"Yeah, Pinky man, your little sister's hot!"

"Who, Iris?" I heard Freddy say.

"Yeah, Iris! Where you been? Check out the titties, man. The chick's got titties."

My heart stopped. And I'd thought it was my sentences they liked! I ran to Mami's dresser, grabbed the bra and, quick as I could, put it on.

Freddy was telling them to shut up, but they kept at it. "Yo, why you getting mad? She can't help it if she's hot, man . . ."

My face was burning.

"Yeah, and did you check out the legs? I think she likes me, too. I'm serious, yo! Anthony, you see the way she kept lookin' up at me?"

"You crazy? She was lookin' at me, not you . . ."

If I'd had my shoes, I would have run out the front door and down the stairs. I might have gone out barefoot, when I heard one of them saying, "I'm gonna go back in and talk to her—" Except then Freddy started shouting at them.

"That's my sister you're talking about! You disrespect her one more time . . . you say a word to her . . ."

Freddy always had a temper. I'd never heard him this mad, though, except with Papi. And these guys must have weighed forty pounds more than him. I didn't know what I was going to do or say, but I opened the door.

They stared at me. Anthony had Freddy pinned by the arms. Freddy's face was bright red as he fought to get away. Mine had to be even redder. "Iris, you heard what they said about you?" he shouted. "Want me to kick them out? I'll kick them out!"

Anthony tightened his hold.

"Yo, yo, Freddy, chill," Kevin said. "Calm down. Relax. We're just playin' with you, man. Nobody's

dissin' your little sister. No need to get all violent!
Right, Iris? We meant it as a compliment." Anthony
nodded. "How old are you, Iris?"

"She's twelve!" Freddy spat it out.

I'd felt so grown up and cool when they were talking with me. I could have kicked myself.

"See, twelve years old and she's already got men
fighting over her. I told you she was hot. No disrespect
intended." Anthony gave me a big grin.

No. They were the ones who needed to be kicked,
being so nice to me one minute, then the next acting
like the guys in front of the bodega, then telling me it's
a compliment.

"Yeah, Freddy man," Anthony was saying now. "You
think we came all the way down here to fight with you?"

"How should I know?" Freddy had stopped shouting.

"If I let you go now, you gonna be cool?"

"Yeah, a'right," Freddy grumbled.

Anthony let go of him and held out a hand. They all
shook. It was over.

And I felt just like I did at school. Like I wanted to
disappear.

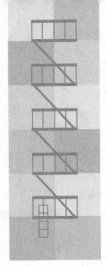

CHAPTER 6

THE WORST PART OF ALL OF THIS, I THOUGHT AS I slunk past them to my room, got my flip-flops, and headed up the fire escape—worse even than being too embarrassed to tell them off, the part that made it even more humiliating and confusing—was that shivery, tingly, bubbly feeling when I was thinking that they liked me. One thing, though. I wasn't going to take any more crap from this peashooter. Or from Brutus, who was growling and snarling as I went by. I'd yell at the peashooter till he told me about Fluffy.

But when I got to his window, someone was already yelling.

"It's always something with you, isn't it, Will? What, do you do this on purpose, to make me late?"

At first I thought it was a woman's voice, it was so high, but when I lay down and peeked under the shade,

I saw a small, scrawny-looking man in green work clothes angrily slapping the mop around the floor. I couldn't see his face, but I could see the boy over by the table, slumped down in his wheelchair. "It's nine already! They dock my pay for bein' late, it's comin' outta your hide, Will!" The man put a curse between almost every word. "I'm sick of this! I don't care if you're a cripple—"

"You can go." The kid sounded scared. "It's okay, Dad. I can finish it."

"And make an even bigger mess? No thanks!" The man leaned the mop against the sink, then checked his watch and cursed again. "I'm outta here . . ."

I had to strain my neck to keep him in sight as he moved toward the kitchen door.

"When'll you be back?" I heard the kid ask.

"I don't know!" the man said.

"After work?"

"Yeah. After work. If they don't fire my ass . . ."

"Right after?"

"I don't know!" The man's voice rose again. "I'll have to see."

"Well, could you, like, bring back a couple of slices of pizza and some Coke?" the boy asked. "And if you stop at the store, some tissues and some juice? We're almost all out—"

The man let out another whole string of curses. "Don't nag me, Will!"

49

"I'm sorry, Dad."

"And this time if something comes up, deal with it, you hear me? And don't be punching in the emergency code on the pager unless it's an emergency. And I mean a real emergency. You keep paging me, Will, I'm gonna throw the pager in the garbage!"

No wonder this kid was shooting things.

The dad was gone. I straightened up and rubbed my knees, which were sore from kneeling on the metal slats. It seemed more and more likely that this kid had shot Fluffy. But it felt too weird now to yell at him the way I'd planned.

I waited as long as I could stand. Then I called, "Excuse me," knocking hard in case he'd left the room. "Excuse me, Will—that's your name, right?—you in there? It's me, Iris, from downstairs. In 2B? Remember, the person you shot and I yelled at you?"

There was no answer, so I kneeled down again and peeked under the shade. I couldn't see him, but I could hear him moving around. "Listen. I don't mean to bother you," I said. "I know I yelled at you before, but this is important. I'm looking for a cat. His name is Fluffy. I haven't seen him since Friday. I'm wondering if you've seen him going by on the fire escape? Or if you maybe shot him? If you shot him, Will, you have to tell me now, okay, so I can find out if he's all right."

I had no clue how I was going to do that, but I hoped it would bring Will to the window.

It didn't. I was sure he was still in the kitchen, though, so I kept talking. "He's, like, this big orange cat with a chewed-up ear and long hair. He could be the Cat Lady's cat. I don't know. All I know is he was coming to see me every day for a week, and I was feeding him, and now he's disappeared."

I suddenly remembered Will telling me how his dad had his dog killed. Maybe it wasn't Will who'd shot Fluffy. Maybe it was his dad.

"Will!" I knocked on the window again. I heard a noise like somebody trying to blow his nose so nobody would hear. "Listen, Will, you know, if there ever *is* an emergency, you could knock on my ceiling. Or bang on the heat riser. I'm always home, you know, Will. I'm not allowed to go anywhere. And I have a big brother. So if you ever need something, we could come right up."

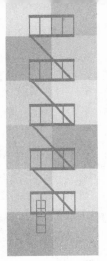

CHAPTER 7

"DON'T EVEN BOTHER TRYING TO BE NICE TO him! They don't want nobody's help." Daisy was out on her fire escape, hanging clothes on a drying rack. "*Mira, chica,* long as you're there, you mind comin' up and giving me a hand?"

I peeked under Will's shade again. He seemed to have left the kitchen.

"*Pyu!* It's so muggy today. The air smells like garbage," she said as I walked up to her landing. She gave me a container of clothespins, and pulled a kid's striped shirt from a dishpan. "Yeah, everyone in the building gave up trying to help them long ago."

"What's wrong with Will?" I asked as I pinned up the shirt, then some socks and a man's boxers. "He can't walk at all? Was he born that way or did he, like, get some disease? How old is he?" Iris, I could hear

Mami's voice saying, you're even nosier than she is! I didn't care. I couldn't leave without knowing. "What's his dad's problem? Where's his mom?"

Daisy dropped her voice. "She passed away."

Oh, no. "What happened to her?"

"Car accident," she whispered. "A couple years ago. The other son died, too."

I put the pins down. "Oh, my God!"

She nodded. "Yeah, and I heard Gladd—it sounds like a joke, right, but that's their real name, Gladd—was drunk. I believe it, too. Everybody loved her. I can't say the same for him, though he was nothing like as bad as he is now. And Will was so good at sports—baseball, basketball, you name it. She was so proud. She got him into a special school, where you have to pass an intelligence test to get in. Now look at him."

This was horrible. "And he's all alone in there? Can he go out?"

"Not without the elevator—"

No wonder he hated seeing me run up and down the fire escape. I almost couldn't blame him if he hated Fluffy for having legs. So maybe it *was* him, and not his dad. "I'm scared Will might've shot the cat," I said. "Or that his dad—"

She nodded. "I know what you mean, honey! Unhappy people like that, anything is possible."

I wanted her to disagree with me.

A cry came from inside her apartment, then a yell, then the sound of kids fighting.

"I gotta go," she said. She put a hand on my shoulder. "*Oye,* Iris, you're a sweet girl, but you try to save every stray cat and everyone with problems, it'll break your heart."

"What about if I just check the roof and the alley and ask everybody in the building?" I said as she climbed in the window.

She turned back. "Forget it. You're not going on the roof. It's too dangerous. And you can't get to the alley except through the basement and you'd have to get Ocasio to let you in. And some of the people in this building, you don't want to mess with. But I'll tell you what. You know Yolanda, *la gordota,* the very large lady? She lives right under the Cat Lady. She's home all day. So's Luisa. They could know something. I'll call right now and tell them you're coming up."

"I haven't seen that cat in a while," Luisa told me in Spanish after she'd scolded me for being on the fire escape again. "But I can't believe Willy could shoot an animal. I used to baby-sit him and his brother when he was little. He was a good boy, very polite, even when he got older. He always helped me carry up the groceries. And he had that big dog he took such good care of. He loved that dog . . ."

That was good news. "What about his dad?" I said.

"I don't like to think about him," she said.

That was bad news.

I went across to 5B, stepping carefully around Luisa's vegetables. I peered around the hanging plant.

"Brrrkkk!"

I did not need this. "Shut up, Cuca," I said. "Nobody's taking your tomatoes."

"Shut up! You shut up!" he squawked.

A woman with orange-yellow hair came to the window. "Just don't call him a dirty bird," she said. "Iris?" She took down the plant so she could see me better.

Daisy was right. She was really large. Young, though, and she looked nice. "Why not?" I said.

"You'll see."

She had such a mischievous look in her eyes that, as upset and worried as I was, I couldn't let it pass. "Cuca's a dirty bird," I said.

"Kiss my little green ass!" screamed Cuca.

"My husband, Tico, has a sick sense of humor," said Yolanda. She moved away from the window and came back with a big green shiny parrot perched on her shoulder. "The only way to Cuca's heart is through his stomach," she said. "Give him a tomato."

I looked at her. "He won't bite me?"

"Just hold your hand out flat."

I picked a tiny one and held it out. I tensed as he flew down and took it from me.

"See, now he likes you," she said as he flew back to her shoulder to eat it. "You ever been kissed on the mouth by a bird?"

I put my hands over my mouth. "No! Eeeoooh!"

She laughed. "Then don't say, 'Dame un besito.' Like I said, Tico is sick. Cuca, say hello, Iris."

"Awwk! Hello, Iris! Shut up, Iris!"

Yolanda shook her head. "This bird loves to tell people to shut up."

I laughed. "He sounds exactly like my fifth-grade teacher. Mrs. Pilcher."

"Oh yeah? 'Cause he looks just like Sister Ursula, my old math teacher. They got the same beak."

It felt good to laugh. Yolanda had a smile that made you smile back, and a way about her that made you think nothing could be as serious as you'd thought.

"So do you know anything about this cat?" I said.

"Only that he walked by all the time. I know 'cause it drove Cuca nuts. Up and down. Up and down. Tico called him Otis for Otis Elevator Company."

"But when was the last time you saw him? Was he going up or down?"

"Up, I think. But I'm not sure."

"And you think he is the Cat Lady's cat."

"Oh, definitely. The only person in this building with cats is the Cat Lady. Even if he started out an alley cat, he'd find his way to the Cat Lady's. Tico says every cat in the neighborhood finds his way to the Cat Lady's. But I haven't seen him lately."

I only had to think about it for a second. "I'm going up."

"By yourself?" She looked at me like I'd said I was going to climb into the polar bear cage at the zoo.

"Well . . . I mean, unless you could maybe, like, introduce me."

"Introduce you?" She let out a laugh. "Number one, I've never even been up there. Two, this is not a normal person. This is *una loca*. Big-time. Three, I don't go up no fire escapes. And neither should you. Four, my kids are sleeping. Do we need more reasons?"

I had more reasons. I hadn't told Freddy where I was going in case Mami called. I'd left the computer on. I was scared. But I had to see. "I won't talk to her," I said. "She won't even know I'm there. I'll be right back."

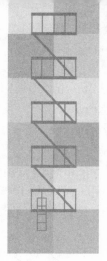

C H A P T E R 8

THE CAT LADY'S WINDOW WAS OPEN A FEW
inches. Two cats sat on her windowsill, the little gray
guy and a lumpy cross-eyed one with black and orange
spots. The gray cat mewed, then came to meet me. "Wish
me luck," I whispered. I walked as far across the narrow
part as I dared, dropped to my hands and knees, crawled
closer and, my heart hammering, peeked in. The cross-
eyed cat jumped down and rubbed against me.

"Can you see anything?" called Yolanda.

"Cats!" I whispered. Walking around, sitting,
sleeping, cleaning their fur—fat cats, skinny cats, pretty
cats, cats that looked like somebody's idea of a joke, a
mother cat with a pile of kittens. "And litter boxes!"
Twenty or so along one wall. Another whole row next to
the sink. A longhaired black cat jumped into one and
started scratching around.

"You see the cat you're looking for?" Yolanda called.

The black cat had a big head and no neck, and was almost as big as Fluffy. Maybe it was his brother. "Not yet."

"Then come down, Iris! Please!"

"Just a second." I heard a creaky, croaky voice sort of like Cuca's. "Yolanda!" I whispered through the slats. "It's her. The Cat Lady's coming!"

Yolanda clambered out her window. "Don't be stupid. Come down from there!"

"I will," I said. "I just want to see what she looks like. She can't see me."

I'd been picturing the Cat Lady all raggedy and bent over, like a bag lady. She was old, but her face was smooth, she was tall, and she had excellent posture. But her voice did sound a lot like Cuca's.

"Thomas, you forgot to remind me to take the grocery list," she said. "Good thing I remembered before I walked down all those steps. You'd have been mad if I came back without your Friskies." The cat she was talking to was the same color as Fluffy but only half as big. I'd seen a few orange cats in here. Could Fluffy be their father? She walked over to the fridge. "What are you doing up on that icebox, Eleanor, trying to stay cool? Maybe I should climb up there with you instead of going marketing. That's right, Hyacinth. Lord have mercy. It's a hot one today."

So then why was her window almost closed, and why did she have on that long-sleeved winter dress with the silver curlicue pin at the collar, and those gloves and that black mushroom-shaped straw hat?

"Now Sweet William"—she went over to the hairy black cat—"can you and Buster Brown get along while I'm gone, or do I need to close Buster in the bedroom? Only reason I let him back in was that you swore to me on the Bible you wouldn't fight, and now here the two of you are, raising a ruckus again, chewing on each other, tearing up each other's ears . . ."

Fluffy had a torn-up ear.

"*Mewp!*" Sweet William sounded just like Fluffy. So then maybe he *was* Fluffy's brother. Which could mean Buster Brown was Fluffy. You'd think Buster Brown would be brown, but if this lady was crazy . . .

The gray cat stepped around me to get onto the landing, put its front paws up on the windowsill, and looked in. Then it meowed really loudly.

"Who's calling me?" said the Cat Lady. "Myrtle, is that you?"

She was coming to the window! She was opening it. I had to get away.

But I never should have tried to scoot back and stand up at the same time. My flip-flop caught under a slat, I lost my balance, flopped across the windowsill, and my glasses dropped onto her floor.

Before I could even catch my breath, the Cat Lady

jumped back and began snatching up cats, screaming, "Run, babies! There is an accursed thing in our midst! Run quickly! Sweet Jesus, they're after us!"

"Iris, what's happening? Should I come up there?" called Yolanda.

"No!" This poor lady already thought she was under attack. "Excuse me. I'm sorry. I'm really sorry," I told the Cat Lady. Those glasses cost two hundred eighty dollars. Mami'd kill me. Not to mention, it was hard to see. I put one leg over the windowsill . . .

"Iris, what are you doing?" yelled Yolanda.

"*Ay, Dios mío! Iris, ten cuidado! Bájate de ahí!*" Luisa must have come out onto her fire escape.

"It's not that girl again? What are you, crazy? Don't go in there!" Oh, my God! Was Mr. Ocasio out on his fire escape, too?

Slowly, slowly I stepped through the window. I couldn't focus well, but well enough to see the Cat Lady picking up a fly swatter. "Get back!" she cried. "Who are you? What do you want with me?"

"Nothing." I put my hands up. The smell in here was horrible. "Just my glasses."

"He's lying, babies! 'Destroy thou them, O God! Cast them out! Babylon the Great is become the habitation of devils and the hold of every foul spirit!'" She waved the fly swatter over her head. "Don't come any closer!"

"I know. I'm not. I'm sorry." Oh, man, did it smell!

"'They that hate without a cause are more numerous than the hairs of mine head!'" She picked up a broom like she was going to whack me with it.

"I don't hate anyone." Keeping one eye on the broom and the other on the fly swatter, I slowly, slowly reached down and snatched up my glasses. "See?" I said. "That's it. That's all. I'm leaving."

But as soon as I put my glasses on, I saw Fluffy. He was fine! Will and his dad hadn't hurt him. "Fluffy!" I called.

"Buster, heed not the voices of evil!" cried the Cat Lady. "Buster, run!"

Fluffy shot past me to the windowsill.

"Fluffy!" I reached for him.

"There's no Fluffy here!" roared the Cat Lady. She swept him off the windowsill with her broom. "Get back in here, Buster! All of you now, run!" Her eyes, when she turned back to me, were blazing. "You're not touching him. You're not touching any of them. And that goes for the inspector, too. You hear that, mister? 'Get thee behind me, Satan! Be gone!'"

I was gone.

"'Though mine enemies should encamp against me, my heart shall not fear,'" she shouted as I scrambled out the window. "'Though war should rise against me, I will be confident. Thy rod and thy staff, they comfort me—'" She shoved the window closed.

I raced across and down the steps to the platform, to where Yolanda was squeezed beside Luisa. I prayed the fire escape could handle all our weight.

"You're lucky you didn't get yourself killed!" hollered Mr. Ocasio. "STAY OFF THE FYESCATE! YOU HEAR ME, IRIS?"

"It's fine, Hector. It's under control." Yolanda practically shoved me through the window into her kitchen, then climbed in after me. Luisa followed.

Even from inside, I could hear Mr. Ocasio shouting. Cuca started hopping in his cage, yelling, "Brrrk! Shut up, Iris! STAY OFF THE FYESCATE! AWWWK! YOU HEAR ME, IRIS?"

"I found Fluffy!" I panted as Yolanda's two curly-headed little boys tugged at her to find out what was going on. "Will didn't shoot him! He's fine."

"You're lucky you're still fine!" Yolanda said. "I thought she was gonna get *you* with that rod and staff!"

"*Tssk tssk.* That poor woman," clucked Luisa. "I thought she was going to have a heart attack. She couldn't figure out if Iris was the health inspector or the devil."

"Yeah, was that the Bible she was quoting or was she making that up?" I asked.

"Got me," said Yolanda.

"She's a very religious woman," said Luisa. "It must be the Bible."

"She's got Fluffy locked up in there," I said. "She may be holding him prisoner—"

"Iris, you're crazier than she is! Here, have a glass of water." Yolanda went over to the sink. "Let's all have a glass of water and calm down."

But before I could calm down, the doorbell rang.

"We know who that is," Yolanda said.

Sure enough, there was Mr. Ocasio, with such a horrible look on his face that Yolanda's boys hid behind her.

"Iris"—he shook his finger at me—"what do I have to do to get you to stay off—"

"She knows!" Yolanda said. "Cuca just told her!"

"It's not funny. She falls off and breaks her neck, her mother's gonna tell the office it's my fault. Next thing I know, I lose my job"—he was getting louder and louder—"she can't be climbing around spying on people, especially crazy people who you don't know what they're gonna do—"

"Excuse me." Yolanda stepped closer to him and held up her hand like she was stopping traffic. "You don't need to raise your voice. And don't be pointing your finger in her face, okay? She's already upset. She wouldn't even be on the fire escape if you'd fix the elevator. . . . You know how long it's been out this time? Thirty-seven days. I'm keeping count."

Mr. Ocasio was not small, but Yolanda made him look petite. He put his finger down.

"And you tell that new manager for me I'm gonna deduct it from my rent," she said. "And I'm gonna advise the rest of the tenants to do the same. Do you know how hard it is for a person my size to go up and down six flights—"

"My son already wrote to the City about how I can't climb stairs," Luisa joined in.

He'd started backing away. "Why you ladies yelling at me? I don't make the rules around here. I'm fifty-eight years old. You think I like hauling garbage up and down? If it was up to me, I'd fix the elevator tomorrow." He made a disgusted sound. "I gotta get back to work. *Mira*, Iris, I'm gonna walk you down, make sure you don't get in no more trouble."

"Go on," Yolanda said. "It's almost eleven. I still got the floors to wash and the groceries to get and chores up to here. Raymond, Andy, let's walk Iris to the door."

"I'm sorry about all this," I told her as we left.

"Are you serious?" she said. "This is the most excitement I've had in weeks. You can come see me anytime. Just don't get everyone crazy. And do yourself a favor. You found Fluffy. Now forget about him. He's no more being held prisoner than Cuca is."

"You need more to do, that's what I think," Mr. Ocasio said as he followed me to my door, his keys jingling with every step. The nasty mix of piss, roach spray, dust, and disinfectant in the stairwell smelled almost as bad as the Cat Lady's. This is why I take the fire escape, I felt like telling him. But he was too busy talking. "What, you just stay in here alone all day while your mother works? She should of sent you to the recreation program over at Our Lady. Or summer school. Or you should baby-sit. You're old enough. *Yo no te quiero ver más en el fyescate!* You got that? Next time, I tell your mother."

"I know," I said. "I won't go up anymore."

Except I really wanted to tell Will about Fluffy.

CHAPTER 9

"*PSST*, WILL!" I PRAYED THE RUSTLING BEHIND
his window shade wasn't him loading up his peashooter. "Don't shoot. I have to tell you something.
You hear me, Will? I'm whispering in case Ocasio's in
his kitchen. I found Fluffy!"

I'd meant to stay off the fire escape at least till Mr.
Ocasio calmed down. But when Mami called, almost as
soon as I got in the door, worried about where I'd been
all morning, I said the first thing that popped into my
head—that I was down doing the wash. So then I really
had to do the wash. And outside the Laundromat I met
Daisy and her grandkids. The two older ones were
nagging her to take them to the sprinkler. So, since I
had nothing to do but go home and type and wait for
Freddy to come home and yell at me about embarrassing him with Kevin and Anthony, I offered to put her

stuff in the dryer and fold it. So now here I was back on the fire escape, bringing up Daisy's clothes.

Will didn't answer, but I was positive he could hear me. "He's fine, Will," I said. "I know you didn't shoot him. He was at the Cat Lady's. And his name is Buster Brown!"

I heard a squeak that could have been the wheelchair. Now what? Apologize? He'd still shot me three times. "I just wanted to let you know," I said. "And tell you I'm dropping off Daisy's laundry, so if you hear someone go by again in a few minutes, hold your fire."

I'd planned to leave the laundry bag outside Daisy's window, then run right down, but she was in her kitchen with the kids. I handed her the laundry bag.

"Thanks a million, honey. You have no idea how much I hate that Laundromat."

She motioned me to come in. I did. "Frankie, *cochino!*" The littlest kid was eating an orange ice pop. "You're dripping icey all over yourself!" She took a napkin and scrubbed his face like he was a dirty pot. "Now I'm gonna have to change your clothes again." She got me a soda from the fridge. "So Iris, I hear you got some scare this morning."

I should have known Daisy would find out about it.

"I guess that's the last time you're goin' up there." She laughed. "That old lady *es bien* crazy, right? Did I tell you she used to give music lessons? I wouldn't send my kids up to her. I wouldn't send anyone up there. I'm just glad you got out of there okay."

"I'm fine," I said. "I found the cat, and he's okay. And I love Yolanda."

"It's a shame, though, how she let herself get so big. Me, I do my exercise tape every morning. Joey, stop it!" She frowned at the other boy, who was going *"Vrooom vroom!"* as he pushed a little car. The girl, who looked five or six, was on the floor, too, eating a red icey and looking through a catalog. "Jessica! Don't eat on my new Avon book." She jumped up and grabbed it away. "This is my business, *mami*, how I make my living. It's not for play." She shook her head again. "I'm telling you Iris, I can't wait for these kids to start back at school. Four more weeks. If my daughter don't hurry up and get her act together, I don't know if I'll make it. How many more weeks till you start school?"

"I don't want to think about it," I said.

"Why? You seem like the type who'd like school," she said. "Glasses and all. Not that they look bad. You're a cute girl even with glasses. Jessica, honey, run and get my wallet. Iris, I want to give you a couple of dollars for bringing up my wash."

"No, that's okay," I started to say. But two dollars was two more than I had now. It would be nice to have a little money. And have something to do outside the house. Daisy wasn't bad, even if it bothered me how she talked about people. "You know," I said, "if you need me to do anything else for you, go to the store, baby-sit..."

"Baby-sit?" She looked up from wiping off the Avon catalog. "Are you serious?"

"Yeah." I nodded. "I like kids. And I help my mom all the time, and I'm excellent at errands, so if you need anything—"

"*Ahorita* no," she said. "*Pero* come back tomorrow morning. Definitely."

I had a job!

"You're not gonna believe this!" I told Will's window on the way down. I had to tell someone. "I just made two dollars. And I'm gonna make more tomorrow." I checked to make sure Mr. Ocasio wasn't at his window. Though he was the one who'd said I needed more to do. "Daisy's got jobs for me. She's gonna pay me! So don't be surprised if tomorrow, you hear me going by again."

And there had to be other people with little jobs for me between now and school! I needed to do something about Brutus, though. This barking was getting out of hand.

It was a little after three when I got home. Freddy still wasn't back, which was good because I was in no hurry to get yelled at, but bad because it'd be better to get the yelling over with before Mami came home. I returned her bra. It'd be good if I was typing when she walked in the door.

The letters on the upper row of keys form
two funny little words: "qwert" and "poiuy."
Memorize them: qwert, poiuy.

I hadn't actually been typing when Anthony and Kevin were over, more like mentally preparing. How hard could it be, though?

QWERT and POIUY came out fine, but THE LASS HAS CASH came out more like TTJE LASSSHS VTSG.

If I asked Luisa and Yolanda tomorrow, I was sure I could line up some jobs.

FGJTYYR FLWWFFfY WYWEYEFGGLUFFY
FLUFF7UY

How did you get this thing to do what you wanted? How did you get rid of letters? If I didn't worry about what finger I used, it worked better.

BBUTRSR , BUTSTR BTUSTER BTUSER,
BUSTER.

Buster wasn't a bad name for him. Papi had this corny thing he used to say when Freddy complained about being calling Pinky. "You can call me anything you like. Just don't call me late for dinner." Fluffy couldn't have liked it at the Cat Lady's or he wouldn't have kept coming here to be with me. I wondered what Will thought when I told him about Fluffy and the Cat Lady. I wondered what time his dad got off work and if he'd bring back a pizza.

> THE LAD IS GLADD. A SAD LAD HAD A BAD DAD. GLADD WAS A BAD DAD.

Hey, I was getting better.

"Iris! Look at you!" Mami dropped her purse, came over, and gave me a big kiss. "You look like a real pro sitting there at the computer! I'm so proud of you! I told you you'd be good at this."

I didn't tell her I'd made up those sentences. Or that I was doing everything Mildred said not to, like typing with my legs crossed and looking at the keys. "Look how stupid this book is," I said, turning to the picture of Mildred at the typewriter. "See, this is the lady who wrote it. And listen to this." I read to her in my Mildred voice:

> "'Asdfg; lkjh dedc frfv gtgb. Let these strange little words haunt you throughout the day and night. Think them into your fingers.

Make them your first waking thought and
your last thought before drifting off to sleep.
Say them as if you were saying your
prayers.'"

"What's wrong with that?" Mami said. "That seems
okay."

"It's stupid," I said. The lock turned. I stopped reading. Freddy walked in the front door and, without a
word, stalked through to his room.

"What's his problem?" Mami said.

"No idea." I really did not want her to find out about
this morning! I began flipping pages.

"'In the world of business, timidity avails
nothing, nor sluggishness, nor lack of
purpose.' 'The raccoon is a cunning little
creature—'"

"I see what you mean," she said. "It is a bit old-
fashioned. Maybe I should get you a real typing program. What could that cost, forty dollars? We can
spend forty dollars on a program—"

I was wondering if I should tell her that soon I'd
have some money to put in, too, when Freddy burst
back into the room. "Forget typing! If you're gonna
spend forty dollars on Iris, get her some bras!"

Mami froze. "What are you talking about? That's not your business. You're embarrassing your sister!"

"She's making it my business! She's embarrassing *me*, Ma! My friends come in here, you think I want them to be laughing, looking at her with her—"

"Shut up!" I shouted.

"Hold on!" Now Mami was shouting, too. "What's goin' on? What happened? What friends are we talking about?"

"Kevin and Anthony." He spit out their names.

"Those punks were over here?" she yelled. "What'd I tell you about hanging out with them? Iris, did those punks say something to you? What'd they say to you?"

She'd go crazy if I told her. "They didn't say anything to me." I couldn't look at her. I couldn't look at either of them.

"Yeah, well, they said plenty to me," Freddy said. "I set them straight, but Ma, it wasn't their fault. If she hadn't of been sitting there with her—"

"No!" Mami cut him off. "Don't gimme that boys will be boys crap. Because I don't want to hear it. Boys may be boys out on the street, but in my house, boys show respect. And that includes you! You get that?"

"I show respect," he shouted. "I show plenty of respect. Not only that, I take all kinds of crap trying to help her out, and she don't even say thank you—"

"Thank you, Freddy," I said under my breath, but he looked too mad to hear me.

"Ma, he was just looking out for me," I tried telling her as he slammed out of the apartment. "Ma, open your eyes! Look at me! Even the lady in 4A told me I need a bra!"

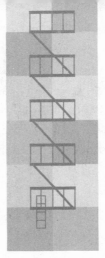

CHAPTER 10

THAT WAS THE WORST THING I COULD HAVE said. Not only did Mami repeat everything she'd said the other night, she repeated it at least five times, each louder than the time before. And then she told me what she thought of *chismosas* who stuck their noses where they weren't wanted, and that if that was the kind of people who lived in this building, she didn't want me talking to them.

I knew she was sorry for yelling, because I overheard her later telling her friends on the phone. I didn't hear anything to make me think she'd changed her mind, though, and she didn't say anything to me, so I didn't ask again.

I typed for a few minutes the next morning and I left the computer on so she could see what I'd done when she got home. Then I put on her bra, looked out the front window, and when I saw Mr. Ocasio hosing off the sidewalk, I ran up the fire escape.

"Brutus, it's just me," I said. "You don't have to go nuts every time I go by." Then, "Hey, Will. Don't shoot. It's me, Iris, off to do my jobs."

Daisy was waiting for me. "I just ran out of paper towels," she said. "And I could use some American cheese and some stamps."

"That's all you need?" I said. I couldn't see charging her for so few things. On the other hand, it meant that I could carry more. I checked Mr. Ocasio's window to make sure he hadn't come home when I wasn't looking, then went up to see Luisa and Yolanda. They both seemed glad to see me, and both gave me a list of things to buy.

This job thing might really work!

"It's me again, Will," I told his window shade on my way down. "On my first shopping trip. I got three customers. You need me to get anything for you?" I didn't really think he'd answer. He didn't.

Mr. Ocasio was out front winding up his hose. I gave him my politest smile and my best good morning.

As soon as I went in, Sammy asked, "You still in the market for a cat? They're on sale again. Free with a ten-dollar purchase."

"No thanks," I said, grabbing a basket.

"Why, you gave up on cats?" he said as he sliced the cheese for Daisy. "Or you found the one you were looking for?"

"Sort of," I said. I was starting to calm down about Fluffy. Not that I didn't still love him and miss having him come and sit with me. And it was a huge relief that he was fine, and that Will hadn't shot him, but I had other things to think about. Like this bra problem. And my new job.

"I'm running errands for people in the building," I said as I picked out Yolanda's apple juice and Luisa's *plátanos* and onions, and the stamps, cheese, and paper towels for Daisy. "Can you ring these three piles up separately? Oh yeah, and how much for a pack of hot dogs?"

"Three sixty-nine," he said.

"No cheaper ones?"

"Cheaper than that, we're talkin' a can of Vienna sausages."

"That won't work," I said. Brutus could eat them, can and all, in one bite. "I'll take the hot dogs."

I cut open the hot-dog package at home, then started up the fire escape. As usual, Brutus grrrred and woofed before I was even halfway up. As usual, only the top of Tattoo Man's window was open, and I thanked God for the glass between me and the dog.

"Yo, Brutus, I got somethin' for you!" I tossed a hot dog in the window. He snapped it up, then licked his lips and stood there looking at me. "Mmm mmm, good. You like that, huh?" I threw him another, then another, then another. This could get expensive. On the other hand, he wasn't barking.

"Did you hear that?" I told Will on my way up to 4. "The sweet sound of silence."

Not only did Daisy tell me to keep the change, she'd also thought of another job for me—watching the kids for a couple hours that afternoon so she could get her hair done.

Luisa had things for me to do, too, but they seemed more like favors than jobs I could charge for. I changed the lightbulb over the sink. I climbed up on a chair and got down a bowl she couldn't reach. I helped open a jar. Then she led me to her bedroom so I could help her find her earring, and showed me pictures of her late husband and her children and grandchildren, and the bedspread and pillowcases she'd crocheted before her hands got messed up from the arthritis.

I crawled around her floor looking for the earring. "You know who used to do these things for me?" she said when I finally found it underneath the dresser. "And watered my plants and helped me clean the fish tank, too, before the accident . . ."

"You're talking about Will?" I wanted to make sure I understood her Spanish.

She nodded. "And if I had an important letter to

read, like from the Social Security or the insurance, he'd translate it into Spanish."

"Will?" I stood up. "Will speaks Spanish? He's not Spanish, though, right? I never heard of any Latinos named Will."

"He's named for his father," she said. "His mother was Dominican."

"I didn't know that!" I couldn't believe Daisy hadn't told me. "You know," I said, "I could translate for you."

We went to the kitchen, and she handed me a letter. "This came last week," she said. "It's from the landlord. I asked Yolanda what was in it, but she said she threw hers in the garbage. She said she doesn't want to hear anything from that cheapskate *comemierda* slumlord until he fixes the elevator."

The letter sounded like it was written by Mildred Dornbush.

It has come to our attention that there are certain problems in the building. . . . Please be assured that we strive constantly to uphold the very highest standards of maintenance and repair. Be advised, however, that we cannot afford to maintain the building at the standards we would wish without the cooperation of all the tenants. Regarding the plumbing, we note that some tenants persist in keeping large

numbers of pets in violation of their lease agree-
ments. Said tenants insist on flushing large
quantities of animal waste material down the
commode, thus causing frequent blockages . . .

I knew "animal waste material" was *caca*, but I didn't
know the Spanish words for most of this, so I sort of
summarized it for her. "What's this about?" I asked.

Luisa frowned. "That poor Cat Lady. They should
stop worrying about her and start fixing the elevator.
What does it say about the elevator?"

I looked down the page.

Hazardous and unsanitary . . . health code violations . . . unless you, the tenants, can bring
pressure, we will be forced to take steps . . .
feel free to address questions to our site management representative, Mr. Hector Ocasio . . .

"Nothing!" I said. "Not one word."

She grabbed the letter from me, crunched it up, and
threw it in the trash. "Yolanda's right. It's not worth
the paper it's written on."

I'd been waiting to ask more about Will, but her
phone rang. And when I got over to Yolanda's with the
groceries, her kids were fighting, so I couldn't ask
Yolanda, either. She did tell me, though, that if I felt

like taking down her laundry the next morning, she could give me a few dollars.

"So I'm in business!" I told Will on my way back down. Of course, he didn't answer. But I was too happy to care, because if I could make, like, five dollars this afternoon baby-sitting for Daisy, and two more tomorrow from Yolanda, and if I kept it up all week, there was no way I would not have enough to buy a bra. Because that's what I was going to do with this money—buy myself a bra. Maybe even two bras.

If I didn't spend it all on hot dogs.

After that first morning, I held Brutus to one hot dog each time I passed by. He wasn't happy about that, but he'd totally stopped barking, and since I passed by at least four times a day every day, he didn't have much to complain about.

There was always something Daisy needed from downstairs. Plus, it went so smoothly when I watched her grandkids that first day, she asked me to watch them for an hour every day so that she could do her exercise tape without them climbing all over her. They whined a lot, but it was okay. I liked Raymond and Andy, Yolanda's boys, a lot better. Yolanda almost always wanted me to stay with them for a half hour so she could have a little break. And Luisa needed my help with all sorts of little things around the house.

You wouldn't think I'd like doing everybody's

chores and errands. Not from all the time I spent not doing my own. These little jobs felt nothing like that, though. Not just because I was getting paid, either, but because of how much everyone here liked me. Okay, not Tattoo Man, but I never saw him, and maybe not Mr. Ocasio, though I had his schedule figured out now, so he didn't see me going by. And probably not Will, even though I still said, "Hello, how you doing," and told him what I was up to every time I passed by.

One time I saw the shade move. Another time I heard little rustling sounds, like he was maybe opening a bag of chips. Another time I heard voices, though the window was closed, so I wasn't sure if it was him and his dad, or just the radio. I never actually saw him shooting pigeons, but a few times, as I was starting up the stairs, I saw the whole line of them suddenly rise up and fly into the air. One morning I was pretty sure I saw his dad coming out of the building. I recognized him by his green work pants and the pissed-off look on his face.

At first I'd asked myself why I talked to Will each time I went by, but then it became part of my routine, like tossing Brutus his hot dog, and making sure Mr. Ocasio wasn't in his kitchen before I scooted past his window, and keeping an eye out for Fluffy, in case he'd managed to escape. I was having a good time—the best time since we'd left the Bronx. I even thought of a name for my business: JUST ASK IRIS.

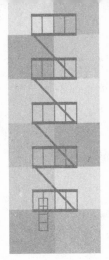

CHAPTER 11

"FREDDY, IS 'WAZOO' A DIRTY WORD?" I CALLED.
I was sitting on my bed, paper, pens, and Magic Mar-
kers spread out around me.

Freddy came in, leaned against the wall, and took a
sip of his soda. We hadn't talked much since the Kevin
and Anthony thing. "Why? What's up?"

I held out the piece of notebook paper:

CHORES UP THE WAZOO?
HATE CLIMBING STAIRS?
NEED HELP WITH ERRANDS, SHOPPING,
YOUR KIDS?
DON'T SAY, "NO, I CAN'T AFFORD IT."
JUST ASK IRIS!

"What do you think?" He didn't know I'd been
doing this. I only went up the fire escape when he was

out, which was more and more, and at times Mami didn't usually call. "I'm going to make a bunch and slip them under people's doors."

He looked at it. "It's cool," he said. "'Just Ask Iris.' I like it."

Great! "So the wazoo doesn't bother you?"

"Nah. But you think anyone will hire you?"

"They already have," I said. "I've been doing it all week—baby-sitting, doing little jobs for people, whatever."

"For real?"

"Uh-huh." I liked the way he was looking at me. Like he was impressed. And like he'd finally stopped being mad.

"And you've been making money?"

I nodded.

"You sneak!" He looked even more impressed. "And you didn't say nothing? So how much have you made?"

"Not that much," I said. "After hot dogs, seven dollars. I don't always charge everyone. There's one lady, Luisa, I don't charge at all. But I need to make at least twenty before school. So I need more customers."

"Whoa. Back up!" he said. "Hot dogs?"

"For Tattoo Man's pit bull," I said. "It's a long story." Several long stories.

"Oka-a-a-y." He squashed his empty can, tossed it across the room into my wastebasket, and sat down next to me. "How do you get more customers?"

"I don't know. Teach Cuca to say, 'Just Ask Iris,' and have him fly around to people's apartments? Maybe that's why they're called 'flyers'?"

"And who's Cuca?"

"The bird upstairs."

"Another long story?"

I nodded.

"You could make those little tear-off tab things with your phone number and post the sign down by the mailboxes."

"No, 'cause then Mami will see it," I said.

"She doesn't know?"

I looked at him. "If it was you, would you tell her?"

"No. So then what's plan B? A beeper? You can't call it 'Just Ask Iris' if they have no way to ask you. And what are you gonna charge?"

"I don't know! That's why I'm asking you," I said. "I just know I can't be wearing Mami's old bra for the rest of my life. And since she's not about to get me one . . ."

Why was it so quiet in here suddenly?

I underlined WAZOO. I added some more question marks.

"That paper you're using looks kind of flimsy," he said. "Let's see what else I can find."

He got some better paper from his room, and for the rest of the afternoon we made flyers, one for every apartment in the building, plus extras. We put the phone number and the hours to call, nine to four, on the bottom corner of each one, and Freddy said he'd help me put them under people's doors. I couldn't wait to get started.

But that night Mami came home sick, and when she tried going in to work Saturday, Graciela told her she couldn't be sneezing and coughing all over the food, and sent her home. So for three days, I was trapped.

Some people like being sick so they can sleep in, read, watch the soaps. Not Mami. It drove her nuts being stuck in bed. She was already upset because Papi had been calling her at work wanting to see her, wanting to talk. And now he'd started calling her at home, too.

"No, I do not need you to come over and take care of me, Pink," she told him. Papi's real name is Arthur, but not even Grandma Lillian calls him that. "Because if you come over here, I'll end up taking care of you, that's why not. So thank you, but forget it." She told him that a bunch of times, but he kept calling.

Each time the phone rang, I ran to the kitchen and picked it up right after she did and then stayed on, waiting for him to ask to see *me* or at least speak to me, but after he'd said, "How are the kids? The kids doing all right?" and she'd told him we were fine, that was that.

"So is he coming, or isn't he?" I heard Graciela ask her one time. I'd started listening in on those conversations, too.

"No, I talked him out of it," I heard Mami say. "But you know as well as I do, this man could say he'd be right over with chicken soup and show up next week with Kaopectate. Or next month with foot powder. Or never show up at all—"

Uh-oh. My nose itched. I felt a sneeze coming. I tried to fight it. *"Aaaaachoo!"*

"Iris, put that phone down!" Mami shouted. "This is not your business."

To me it was, but after that I made sure to pick up the phone very slowly and always keep my hand over my nose and mouth. It was listening to those conversations that convinced me I could get old and die waiting for her to get me a bra. That was definitely my business.

Somewhere in all this, Mami realized that from the pullout sofa in the living room, where she slept, she had a perfect view of the computer screen. "Iris, come in here," she called to me. "Let's do a little typing."

"Do I have to?" I said.

"Do you have something better to do?"

Not with her around.

Asdfg; lkjh dedc frfv gtgb
Asdfg; lkjh dedc frfv gtgb

CHO;RES UYP THE WAZU9!!!!!!!!!!
THE LASS NEEDS CASH!!!!!!!!!!!!!!

She seemed to think that if only I could type, *poof!* all my problems would go away. Which was the way I was starting to feel about the bra.

The raccoco,m is a ;cunning littttle tcretaoure and vveyrry=cleaean.

"I hate this book!" I said. "It's driving me insane."
"I know, I know," she said. "And as soon as this flu's over, we'll get something better."

Mrs. Goerge Grunt is a freind of mrs. Ezra Q. Bixby, JR.

Mrs. qilliam w;. Mollidmilloopi wore jer new new bllue hat tto luncheom.

The suicccessfl businyss ezrecutive is a quietly dressed, soft-sploken well-mnanerd man wso is corrretc in every detail.

"Mrs. Ezra Q. Bixby?" I said. "Man?" I read her the sentences. "Ma, this is so sexist. I can't type this. It's, like, from the Middle Ages!"
I could see she agreed with me, because she

said, "Okay. Fine. You want to do something? Buy us some more orange juice. And see if Sammy has cold pills."

I was so glad to be free, I hardly cared that the bra was in her drawer, where I couldn't get to it. I threw on the trusty overshirt and went down to the bodega.

"Iris, guess who was just in here?" Junior said when I went in. "*La loca*. The Cat Lady. You shoulda seen the hat she had on today—"

"So he asks her, 'What's that, your tutti-frutti hat?'" Sammy said. "Because it had these bunches of fruits on it—berries, cherries, grapes, what have you. She told him it was her good luck hat."

"'Young man'"—Junior went into his Cat Lady voice—"'good things always happen when I wear this hat.' That's what she said—"

"Yeah, and then she asks him to bring up fifty pounds of cat litter—"

"And I'm, like, 'No problem, ma'am, soon as they fix the elevator.' And then she's, like, 'If you carry it up the stairs for me, I'll give you a piano lesson.'"

Sammy chuckled. "That was because one time when Junior went up, she was playing the piano—"

"And I made the mistake of asking her what it was and she said, 'That's Mozart, young man, the great Wolfman Something-or-other Mozart. Do you enjoy Mozart?'"

They were both laughing.

"I could offer to carry up the litter for her," I said.

"You better take a clothespin for your nose!" Junior said. "Or a gas mask."

"She better take some catnip!" Sammy said.

"Maybe I will," I said.

They thought I was joking till I went over to the pet section, came back with a big jar of catnip, and plunked down my $2.29. "Hey," I said, "you never know."

Now they really thought I'd lost my mind. But if it got another job for Just Ask Iris, and it gave me a way to see Fluffy . . . and it wasn't like I'd be going up by myself. Freddy had already promised he'd help hand out the flyers.

As soon as I got home, I added two new lines to each of them.

CARRYING HEAVY PACKAGES?
TAKING CARE OF PETS?

It was even harder, after that, to wait for Mami to go back to work. But finally, she did.

I had the flyers spread out on the kitchen table, making a few last improvements while I waited for Freddy to wake up and come out with me, when I heard the banging—a loud *Thump! Thump!* from overhead.

Thump! Thump! There it was again.

First I thought Mr. Ocasio must be working on the pipes in Will's kitchen. But it sounded more like somebody was thumping on the floor. Had Will fallen out of his wheelchair and started dragging himself across the room? That would have been soft thumps. These were loud, and sharp, more like *Bam, bam, bam!*

Then I remembered. I'd told Will to knock if he ever needed me.

I put on Mami's bra and ran up the fire escape. Brutus whimpered. He couldn't believe I had no hot dogs for him. Tough luck, Brutus.

When I got to Will's landing, the window was open and the shade was up. I looked in, but it was so bright out, I couldn't see much. Heart pounding, I climbed in the window.

"Will?" I called. It smelled kind of garbagey in there. "Will, are you all right?"

"What took you so long?" he said, wheeling himself in from the other room. "I was banging and banging. I'd given up!"

"Are you okay?" I said. He looked okay, or as okay as he'd looked the other times. "What's happened? Is something wrong? What's up?"

"Nothing," he said. "I just thought you'd want to know. I saw your cat."

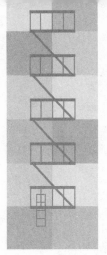

CHAPTER 12

"THAT'S WHAT YOU WERE BANGING FOR?" I SAID.
"I thought it was an emergency!"

"Well," he said, "you were coming by all the time and
then you stopped. What happened? You made enough
money, or you gave up?"

"I didn't give up." He never answered me, anyway,
so what was his problem? "I couldn't leave," I said.
"My mom was sick. She doesn't know I come up here.
She doesn't like me talking to people."

"My dad doesn't even like me talking to him," Will
said.

The smell in here was like old cigarette butts mixed
with that canned-vegetable-and-old-milk-carton-
school-lunchroom smell—not so strong you had to
hold your nose, but if you had a can of Lysol, you'd
have started spraying. There was spaghetti dried onto

the plates piled up in the sink, a foil pie plate with the last blobs of lemon meringue pie on the counter, a pizza carton and soda cans sticking out of the garbage bag in the corner. And that was just some of the mess.

At least Will wasn't a mess. His hair hung down in his eyes but it seemed clean, and he had on a clean T-shirt and tan pants. I hadn't gotten a good look at his legs before. I'd been wondering what they looked like, or if he even had legs. He did, and except for how they were sort of bent toward one side, they just looked like legs.

"You really saw Fluffy?" I said.

"Yeah! A few minutes ago."

He wheeled himself next to me. The only other time I'd seen him up close, he had this tight, pinchy look, like he spent all his time thinking mean, angry thoughts. It's not that he was smiling now, but he'd, like, perked into life. "I was right here," he said, "waiting for this pigeon to get close enough so I could get a shot at him? And see that big branch"—he pointed out the window—"it started shaking, like there was something in there. First I thought it was a squirrel. Then I saw it was Fluffy! He looked like he was after something. Or something was after him. You shoulda seen him run along that branch! Then he jumps down to the next branch and then he's, like, *fooooomm!* headfirst down the tree! I never saw a cat do that! The Cat Lady may have been trying to keep him locked up, but he's out now, and that cat can move!"

"So then you did hear me talking to you," I said. "I knew it!"

"But even if I didn't," he said, "I'd know his name was Fluffy 'cause of all the times I heard you going, 'Heeeeere, Fluffy! Come on, Fluff, Fluff! Where are you, Fluffernut?'"

He made it sound so much like me, I had to laugh.

"Your balcony's right downstairs, remember?"

I laughed again, hearing him call the fire escape a balcony, like we lived on Park Avenue or in a castle.

"Anyway," he said, "I didn't see him come back up, so if you want to find him, you should check the alley right now. You can go through my house and down the stairs. It's faster than going back through your house. Oh, man, I hope he's still down there!"

He started toward the next room. I followed him. His wheelchair wasn't one of those big, heavy, black motorized ones, with the, like, joystick, that you sometimes see people driving down the sidewalk. He had to make the wheels go with his hands.

"My room, in case you were wondering," he said.

"It's right above my room," I said. His room was neater than mine. The bottom bunk was made, but the top one had a bare mattress. Had that been his brother's, or did Will sleep up there before the accident? The desk had a computer on it with some kind of game running, a printer, a big stack of books, and a neat pile of magazines. The bed in the next room looked like it hadn't been made in weeks. There were clothes and newspapers on the floor, a smelly ashtray, and a couple of glasses on the bedside table with brown stuff that looked like old booze. The living room was neater, probably because nobody used it much, and the furniture looked pretty nice, but it could have used a shot of air freshener.

Will unlocked the front door and moved aside, but as I stepped through, he cursed. "I just remembered!" he said. "You can only get to the alley through the basement, and you can't get to the basement without the elevator . . ."

I was disappointed, but he looked *really* disappointed. Disappointed and mad. "It's okay," I said. "He might not even be down there."

He cursed again.

"Don't worry about it," I said. "Everyone's saying I need to ease up on the Fluffy thing, anyway. I mean, we know he's okay, right—"

"And you're developing this close, personal relationship with Brutus, feeding him all the hot dogs. I do not want to smell your pockets—"

"I told you about the hot dogs?" I said.

"Uh. . . ." He went back into his Iris imitation: "'Good pit bull. Nice doggie. Okay, I'll give you one more hot dog. But just one, right? I'm not giving you six. Oh, okay. Here's another.'"

I made a face. "Did I really sound that stupid?"

He went back to his real voice. "How many do you give him?"

"Only one per trip."

"One up, one down?"

I nodded.

"And how many trips per day? Never mind. I know how many." He cursed. "That is one spoiled, lucky dog."

"I have to do something to keep him from going bananas every time I pass by," I said. "I'm trying to get my business going. 'Just Ask Iris.' What else can I do?"

"You never heard of dog biscuits? This is a dog, right? Dogs eat dog biscuits. Dog food. Dog chow. Dog yummies. Hot dogs are for people." He was getting that flat, bitter look again, that pigeon-shooter look.

First he totally ignores me, then it's like he's all involved trying to find this cat for me, like we're old friends, getting me to like him, and then he's mad? I didn't get it.

He cursed the elevator. I got it. "How do you get down without the elevator?" I said, trying to keep my eyes off his legs.

97

"Duh. I don't." His face looked like Freddy's did around Papi. "Not unless my dad takes me down. . . ."

"Oh." Being carried down the steps by Will's dad didn't sound too good. But, then, being stuck up here was even worse. I knew a little about being stuck.

"I don't know what I'm going to do when school starts," he said.

"Hey, not going to school would be fine with me," I said. "If I couldn't go to school, it wouldn't bother me a bit." I saw instantly that was the wrong thing to say. But what was the right thing? How was I supposed to act with him—pretend I hadn't noticed he was crippled? Were you even supposed to call it "crippled"? Did it hurt? How did he go to the bathroom? What was it like for him in school? My head buzzed with questions I couldn't ask.

"Just ask Iris what?" he said after we'd stayed there for what seemed like minutes without either of us saying a word.

"Anything," I said. "You know. Anything anyone needs help with, I'll do it."

Now his face had closed down totally.

"Well, I guess I'll go," I said. "I have to see if my brother's up. So we can go hand out my flyers. . . ."

Freddy was still sleeping when I got home. I was trying to decide whether to wait or go out without him when I heard more thumps on Will's floor.

I wasn't that ready to get into anything with him again. But if he'd seen Fluffy . . .

Brutus couldn't believe I was going up a second time with nothing for him.

"You know—" Will still had that pinchy, angry look, but now he looked kind of nervous, too. Nervous or shy. "We have some dog biscuits. You can have them if you want." He hadn't mentioned Fluffy.

"Won't your dad mind?" I said.

"Hey, I'll tell him I ate 'em," he said. "It's not like we're getting another dog anytime soon. He won't care." He went over and opened the metal cabinet beside the sink. I could see Ramen noodle packets, a box of mac and cheese, onion soup mix, and a big blue box of Milk-Bones. He pulled it out. FOR LARGE DOGS, the box said.

I'd vowed I was never going to ask him another question, but out it popped: "What kind of dog was he?"

"She. Poodle. A standard. My mom's." He shook the box. "It's almost full, so if you want 'em, take 'em." He wheeled himself over to the window and handed it to me.

"Thanks," I said.

"No problem," he said. "If I see Fluffy again, should I knock?"

"That'd be good," I said. "As long as it's before four, when my mom gets home." Then I had an idea.

"Listen." I knew he might get mad again, but I said it, anyway. "I was thinking about what you said about the hot dogs . . ."

"Oh, yeah?" he said.

"Yeah. I still have a few left," I said. "I could come up another time, if you want, and maybe *we* could eat them."

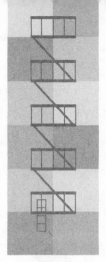

CHAPTER 13

"YO, MAN, IT STINKS IN HERE!" FREDDY FANNED
the air as we headed up the stairs. "Whoooh! When was
the last time anybody cleaned this place?"

"Why do you think I never come up this way?" I
said. "Why do you think I use the fire escape?"

"I'm not going up here," he said. "It smells too bad!"

"Then hold your nose. Come on, Freddy, please!"
I said. "I've been waiting since Friday to do this. I
need more customers so I can get a bra. You're taking
me to get one, right?"

"Me? No." He stopped walking. "No way."

"You're supposed to look out for me and take me
anywhere I need to go," I reminded him.

"Not to get no bra! Nuh-uh." He shook his head.
"I'm doing these flyers with you, but the rest is ladies'
business. No, no! I don't do underwear."

"Okay, okay." There was no point pushing it before I had the money, anyway.

I slipped a flyer under Tattoo Man's door. "I'm going to be brave and give him one even though he hates me."

Freddy pointed to 3B. "Who lives in there?"

"A kid," I said. "His name is Will."

"Does he hate you, too?"

"No." He'd looked really happy when I'd suggested eating the hot dogs. "I think we may be sort of friends. I'm not sure." But even if Will and I were friends, there was no way his dad would ever give me a job, so I didn't leave them a flyer.

I decided not to leave one for Mr. Ocasio, either. "I'm brave, but I'm not stupid," I told Freddy.

I couldn't decide, when we got to the top floor, if it was brave or stupid to ring the Cat Lady's bell. I could hear the TV going in the other apartment. I knew someone named J. Gordon lived here, because I'd seen it on the mailbox downstairs, but that was all I knew. Nobody had said anything to me about any J. Gordon.

"We'll do this one first," I told Freddy. "Stay next to me." Then I rang the bell.

J. Gordon turned out to be an old guy wearing a Yankees cap and thick, yellow-tinted glasses.

"Eye contact," that's what Papi always said was the

salesman's secret to success. Not that I was a salesman or Papi was successful. "Good morning, Mr. Gordon." I looked him in the eye. "You need anything from the store? Or help with anything?"

"Not 'less you know how to fix elevators," he said. "I'm off work today, so I picked up everything I need."

"Well, if you ever do need help . . ." I gave him my best Mildred Dornbush smile and handed him the flyer.

He studied it. "Which one of you's Iris?"

"That would be me," I said, before he shut the door.

Freddy snorted. "He's either blind or thinks he's funny. Let's go."

"Not yet." I fingered the jar of catnip in my pocket. Then I pressed the Cat Lady's bell. We waited. I put my ear to the door. Nothing. Just a few meows. *Bzzzzzt!* I tried one more time.

The peephole opened. I motioned Freddy to move over so she couldn't see him. "Who's there?" she called in that creaky, croaky voice.

"It's Iris," I said. "Iris Pinkowitz." So she couldn't think I was Satan or the health inspector, I added, "The little girl from 2B."

"Little girl?" Freddy raised an eyebrow.

I clamped my hand over his mouth. "I'm helping people in the building."

"I don't need help," she said.

"Also," I said, "I like your cats."

The chain lock rattled. The floor lock clanked. The latch turned. The door opened about six inches. "Get back, babies," I heard her say. "This may be trouble."

I shot Freddy a look. He moved back into the corner.

She was wearing the same dress I'd seen before, with the same pin. Her gray hair, frizzly around the edges, was pinned on top of her head in braids. No hat. That felt like a good sign. She didn't always wear her hat and gloves.

Her eyes narrowed. "How do you know my cats?" she said.

I made eye contact. "I see them sometimes, that's all, out on the fire escape. When I'm up here helping Luisa and Yolanda. But"—Was it possible she didn't remember me? And was that good, or was it another sign she was crazy?—"the only one of them I really know is . . . Buster Brown."

"Buster Brown?" She glanced back into the apartment. "What do you want with Buster Brown?"

"Nothing," I said. "He's a great cat. I really like him. But . . ."

"But what? What's Buster done now?"

"Nothing," I said.

"That cat's already got me in too much trouble," she said. "With the superintendent, with the man next door, and now last week that rude man in 3A with the vicious dog told me if he lays eyes on Buster again, if I don't keep that cat locked up, which I have been doing—"

That was weird. "He's locked up now?"

She glanced back again. "He better be."

Less than an hour ago, Will told me he'd seen him running by.

I handed her a flyer. She took her glasses from her pocket and put them on. "'CHORES UP THE WAZOO?'" she read. It sounded so funny in her creaky Cuca voice, but I didn't laugh. I was remembering how Will's dad had accused Will of beeping him so he'd come home from work. So maybe Will hadn't seen Fluffy. Maybe he'd lied. "'HATE CLIMBING STAIRS?'" She read on. "'NEED HELP WITH ERRANDS, SHOPPING, YOUR KIDS? CARRYING HEAVY PACKAGES? TAKING CARE OF PETS? DON'T SAY, "NO, I CAN'T AFFORD IT." JUST ASK IRIS!' Hmmph." She took off her glasses and looked me up and down. "And you say you're Iris?"

I nodded. "I can do chores, help out with cats, carry up food, or carry down your Kitty Litter—"

She frowned. "No, thank you. My babies and I manage just fine."

"I understand. Maybe you'd like this, though." I reached into my pocket and held out the jar of catnip.

"I don't have a cat, so I don't need it."

At first I didn't think she'd take it. But, after look-ing it over, reading the label, opening it up, and sniffing it, she did. "My babies will appreciate this," she said. Then she closed her door.

"I did it! I met the Cat Lady!" I pounded Freddy on the shoulder as we started down the stairs. "She wasn't even that scary. Not like the—"

A black dog ran past us, ran down two more flights, then raised his leg.

"Yo, yo, cut that out!" Freddy shouted. "Look at that, Iris! He's peeing on the wall! No wonder it stinks so bad in here. He's using our building as his dog toilet." We looked up. Mr. Gordon's door was open again. "I'm going up and talk to that joker."

"No, wait a minute," I said. "Don't piss him off, okay? Let's think about this."

"Why? The guy's a jerk." Then his eyes bright-ened as he saw what I was getting at. "That's good. That's very good, Iris. There's a business opportunity here."

The dog finished peeing, ran back up the stairs and in Mr. Gordon's door. We followed him and rang the bell.

"What can I say?" Mr. Gordon shrugged. "I tell him to go down to the street, but he's an old dog. He gets tired. Now if they'd fix the elevator—"

"Well," Freddy said, "remember Just Ask Iris?"

"That's right," I said, giving Mr. Gordon my Mildred Dornbush smile again. "I can take him down for you, walk him around the block, give him some exercise . . ."

He looked at me. "How much you charge?"

"How much you want to spend?" Freddy asked.

"Nothing," said Mr. Gordon. "I thought you said she was Iris."

I could see Freddy fighting to keep his smile on his face. "How 'bout a dollar a walk?"

"How 'bout fifty cents?" said Mr. Gordon.

Freddy was looking at him like, how 'bout I kick your ass, but he didn't say anything. So I waited, though I was thinking, two walks a day, let's see, at fifty cents a walk and—I'd been counting—twenty-three days, including weekends, until school . . ."

"Okay, seventy-five cents," said Mr. Gordon. "I leave for work at eight-thirty. You can start tomorrow morning."

"Tomorrow's good," I said. Mami left at ten to eight. "I'll be here at eight."

Mr. Gordon nodded. "His name's Blackie."

"Yeah, that's original," Freddy said as soon as Mr. Gordon closed his door, but he smiled as I slapped him five.

"I should tell Ocasio I just solved his cleaning problem," I said as we went down the stairs. "I should get him to pay me, too, for keeping his hall clean."

"Go ahead," Freddy said.

"I was joking," I said. "He already hates me." We were right outside his door now. "Besides, he won't be home."

"You won't know unless you ring," Freddy said. "And if he already hates you, what's the difference?"

I rang. Mr. Ocasio came to the door.

"H-e-e-e-y, how you doin'?" said Freddy. If I was Mildred Dornbush, he was Papi.

"Good morning. Hello. You need any help with anything, Mr. Ocasio?" I looked him in the eye and handed him a flyer. "I can get you things from downstairs if you want. Or go to the store for you, what have you. Just Ask Iris."

"Nah, there's nothing I need," he said. "I'm all set."

"You told me I needed more to do," I said. "So I'm helping people around the building."

"Yeah, first time is free," Freddy said. "After that, you can pay her anything you think's fair."

"Okay, let me think about it," he said. "Come back tomorrow."

We laughed the whole way to our door. "I knew that free thing would get him," Freddy said.

"So are you, like, my agent or something now?" I asked him. "I don't have to, like, pay you a fee, do I?"

"Not yet," he said. "We'll see what develops. Iris, you're going to get a nice business going. And if the elevator stays broken until school starts, yo, you can really rake in the dough!"

"Yeah!" I was so happy. But I'd have been a lot happier if he'd said he'd go with me to buy the bra. And if I understood what was going on with Will and Fluffy.

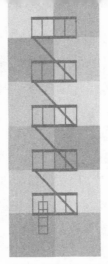

CHAPTER 14

I DIDN'T GET TO SEE WILL UNTIL THE NEXT morning, after I'd walked Blackie.

"This young lady's gonna take you for a real walk today," Mr. Gordon said as he snapped on Blackie's leash. "Ready to go, boy?"

Blackie was ready. "Good boy! That's right. Keep going," I said as he pulled me down the stairs. But the instant he got to the third floor, he lifted his leg. "No, Blackie! Bad dog. That's wrong. No, please, Blackie! Blackie, don't do that!" I yelled, yanking on the leash. But it was too late. And of course Mr. Gordon was listening. But I did what I promised and walked Blackie around the block. And after I handed him back to Mr. Gordon and took care of the puddle, I put a few more Milk-Bones in my pocket and went up the fire escape.

Will must have been waiting by the window. "I'm still looking for Fluffy," he said when I got over there. "I haven't seen him since yesterday."

What a shock. "I doubt you will see him," I said. "The Cat Lady told me she's keeping him locked in the house."

He looked surprised, then puzzled, then angry. "You're saying I'm lying?"

"No, I'm just trying to understand," I said.

"No, you think I'm lying. My dad always thinks I'm lying, too! I'm not, Iris. I swear to God. The cat ran by that time. I saw him!"

Maybe it was the look in his eyes—like he knew nothing he said would make any difference. Or maybe I couldn't stand having him think I was like his dad. Or maybe I just wanted to believe him. "I don't think you're lying," I said.

We had one of our usual long silences when I tried to figure out if I should stay or leave. Finally he said, "How'd Brutus like the biscuits? You gave them to him just now, right?"

"He gobbled them as fast as I could throw them in," I said. Then I said, "Will, you know the big black dog in 6A, with the hairy tail?"

"The one that pees outside my door? My dad's threatening to kill that dog."

"Yeah, well, I'm supposed to be doing something about that," I said. "But I need your advice. I don't know how to get him to keep walking. You had a dog. What should I do?"

"You have to train him," Will said. "Show him the biscuit, then take him off his leash and run down ahead of him. When you get to a landing, hold out the biscuit. Lure him down."

"Will that work?"

He shrugged. "No clue. But, hey, if it doesn't, next time ring my bell on your way up to get him, and I'll be ready with my peashooter." There was a gleam in his eye. "One pea and I guarantee, he won't be pissing on the stairs. I've been wanting to catch that dog in the act for so long . . ."

I laughed.

"So did you seriously talk to Ms. Witherspoon?" he asked.

"That's the Cat Lady's name?"

"Yeah. Ms. Witherspoon. For real? You talked to her?"

"I gave her a flyer," I said.

"And she opened the door for you?"

"Uh-huh." I nodded.

"You weren't scared?"

"Why would I be scared?" I didn't tell him Freddy was with me.

"My brother went up one time when he was selling magazine subscriptions, and he said she started, like, yelling stuff from the Bible, saying how he couldn't take away her cats. He ran down the stairs so fast—"

"She wasn't like that with me," I said. "I even brought her a little present."

"But you didn't see Fluffy—"

"*Oye*, Iris, is that you down there?" Daisy was leaning out her window. "Where you been, *chica?* I been spoiled having you come up here every day. Come on up. I need to just ask Iris something—"

"I've got to go," I told Will. "I'll try what you said. I'll tell you if it works."

"My peashooter's all ready," he said. "Just say the word."

"Listen, can you watch these kids for a while?" Daisy said when I got up there. "I can't get nothing done with them hanging on me all day long."

"My mom was sick," I said.

"Well, it's a good thing she's better," she said, "because I'm starting to go nuts."

So I read to her grandkids while she got some chores done and showered and exercised, and then I took the fire escape up to Yolanda's and knocked on her window.

She was even happier to see me than Daisy was. "Oh, Iris," she said, "I've been praying you'd come by and take these kids off my hands. They threw up the whole weekend, and Tico's working overtime this week, and I don't like to keep asking Luisa to watch them, and they're fine now, but it's getting to the point where—"

"My mom was sick," I said. "You want me to take them to the playground?"

"No! I'm the one who needs to get out of here," she said. So while she went for a walk, I pushed cars and trucks around with Raymond and Andy and taught Cuca to say "ee-i-ee-i-oo" when we sang "Old MacDonald." When she got back, we all had cookies and sandwiches. Then I knocked on Luisa's window to see if she had any jobs for me.

Instead of Luisa, Mr. Ocasio appeared in the window with a wrench in his hand. I was ready to run, but he said, "Got a job for you if you still want one. You can run down to the hardware store for me and pick up a flushometer for this toilet."

He wasn't yelling at me for being on the fire escape? I didn't know what a flushometer was, but he gave me the old broken one to take with me and told me to charge it to the building, and when I was back at Luisa's window with the new one in ten minutes, he almost smiled.

After Mr. Gordon came home that afternoon, I did what Will said with Blackie and the dog biscuit. I had to scramble to stay ahead of him on the stairs, but I did, and he made it to the second floor.

"That's progress," Will said when I told him. He was the cheerfulest I'd seen him.

I was cheerful, too. I'd made five dollars that day.

By the end of the week, I had thirteen dollars, Blackie was peeing by the hydrant, and Freddy was saying, "You better watch out! I may have to just ask Iris for a loan!"

Mami still didn't know about my business. I made sure I was home for her daily lunchtime call and called her a couple times a day, in case she'd built up any urge to talk to me. And I was pretty sure she still didn't know I was wearing her bra. Not that anyone in the building cared. I could have gone up in my pajamas and they'd have been happy to see me. Even Mr. Ocasio stopped caring that I was going up and down constantly. "Because that way he gets to send me to the hardware store whenever he needs anything, which is all the time," I told Will.

Will knew about all of this. Except, of course, the bra. I stopped to talk to him for a minute or two almost every time I went by. He kept the shade up now, and seemed to always be in the kitchen.

But there was still the Fluffy question. Until one afternoon, after I'd finished walking Blackie, I heard the sound of locks turning on the Cat Lady's door.

"Excuse me," she said, opening the door a few inches. "Are you the young lady who wants to be asked to do things for people?" She had on the same dress with the same curlicue pin, but she was wearing socks and house slippers instead of those big old shoes and heavy stockings. And no hat. A bunch of cats crowded around her legs.

"Yes, ma'am," I said. "That's me. Iris."

"Well, Iris," she said, closing the door to just a crack to keep two kittens from running into the hall. "I'm sorry to bother you. I seem to have mislaid my glasses. I've turned the house upside down, and try as I might, I can't find them, and I can't do a thing without them."

"Would you like me to help?" I tried not to look too excited.

"Yes, please," she said, "if it's not too much trouble."

Wait till Will heard about this!

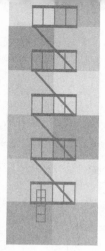

CHAPTER 15

POW! THE SMELL HIT ME THE INSTANT I STEPPED through her door. The Cat Lady's nose must have given up and died years ago. I'd have held mine, except it would have hurt her feelings. I could see she was trying to keep her house clean—her little knick-knacks were dusted, she'd covered the couch and chairs with sheets, and she had one of those old carpet cleaners like Grandma's standing in the corner—but there was no way. Not with cats on the windowsill, cats on the bookcase and the sofa and the chairs, cats sleeping on the rug. No sign of Fluffy, though.

A black cat with white feet had been lying underneath the fringy lampshade like it was a beach umbrella. It jumped down off the table and began checking me out.

"Boots, you bad boy, did she tell you she wants you sniffing at her?" the Cat Lady scolded him. "Iris, if I didn't know better, I'd think those glasses had grown legs and walked away just to torment me. I can't read my Bible, I can't sew, I can barely read my music . . ."

They weren't on any of the furniture, so I started looking under things. A bunch of cats came over to see what I was doing. A goofy-looking black cat came over and poked his nose in my face.

"Ronald, who's this on the floor?" she asked him. "You'll have to excuse Ronald. He's a teenager," she told me. "He's about to go in for his operation. The first of every month, when I get my check, I bring one of the young ones over to the clinic. Two, when I can afford it. I try to get them fixed before they start to spray or come into heat . . ."

A cockroach scurried across the floor in front of me. I jumped up just as two cats dived for it. "No glasses under there," I said.

I followed her to her bedroom. Except for the cats and the smell, so far this didn't look like a crazy person's house, just an old person's. I'd have liked to get a better look at her little ballerina statues, and the old yellowy photos tucked into her pictures of Martin Luther King Jr. and JFK. Her dresser had one of those silver brush and comb sets, a wig stand with a black wig on it, a bunch of hairpins, and some fancy, old-fashioned perfume bottles on a wooden tray. No glasses. The glasses weren't on the bookcase, either.

"That's the Professor, Miss Lucy, Mickey, Minnie—on account of the ears—Ike, Bo Peep . . ." The Cat Lady introduced the cats curled up on her bed. Where was Fluffy?

"Don't you run out of names?" I asked.

"That's half the fun," she said, "coming up with names. I named my first ones for the presidents of the United States and their First Ladies, but not all of them can handle a name like that. Like this skittery one I call Jitters because everything scares her. You have to match names with personalities. See"—she pointed to an old, cross-eyed white cat—"now there's one with the wrong name. Ulysses S. Grant. But I was afraid if I changed it, I'd hurt his pride. You have to respect their dignity, and you never want to insult their intelligence. Of course, some aren't as intelligent as others. . . ."

Her glasses were right on her night table, wedged between the tissue box in its crocheted cover and her Bible. I didn't say anything, though, because I could just hear Will saying, what, you left without seeing Fluffy? "Excuse me," I said. "Where's Buster Brown?"

"Buster?" She looked up from petting President Grant. "In the closet, most likely. Now where in the world could those glasses be? I already looked on the music stand, but I guess it can't hurt to look again." She led me into the next room, which had an old piano on one wall, and opened the closet door. "Buster Brown, you in there? He spends all day in there sulking because I have him locked up in the house. He got out last week for a little while when I wasn't looking—"

"He did?" So then Will really had seen him!

"He most certainly did! And now he's so down in the mouth, he won't talk to anyone. He even stopped beating up on Sweet William. Buster, baby, come on out, you got a visitor."

And out came Fluffy, blinking his eyes, stretching, looking—except for the bell around his neck—exactly like he always did. I didn't know if I was happier to see him or to know Will had been telling me the truth. I'd wanted to believe him, so I'd believed him, but something inside me relaxed knowing it for sure.

I picked Fluffy up and buried my face in his neck. He started to purr.

"I'm glad to see he's cheering up finally," the Cat Lady said.

I didn't dare remind her Fluffy and I were old friends.

"Well, you're meeting my babies, Iris, but we're not doing too well finding my glasses. I had them on when I was washing out my hose"—she led me to the bathroom— "Lord knows, I've already looked in there, but . . ."

The bathtub was full of plastic grocery bags of used

Kitty Litter. The smell made my eyes sting and brought my nose back to life. Even Fluffy ran as soon as we walked in. "Uh, let's check the bedroom again," I said. "Oh, look! There they are!" I shouted as soon as we got in there.

"Lord have mercy," she said as I handed her the glasses. "Thank you, sugar. I must have looked there a dozen times."

"Except you didn't have your glasses on," I said, picking up Fluffy, who'd come in after us, "so it was hard to see them." The clock on the table said 4:00. "I have to go," I said. "My mom will be looking for me."

Fluffy let me carry him all the way to the front door.

"I'd like to give you a little something for your trouble," the Cat Lady said. "How much do I owe you?"

"Nothing." I nuzzled Fluffy. "It's fine." I had twenty dollars already, and there was still nineteen days till school. "You don't owe me anything. In fact, you need me to do anything else for you? I could take some of those bags of litter down for you now, or carry up food . . ." Or buy you some cockroach spray and some Lysol. I didn't say that.

"I don't carry the litter out," she said. "That super can holler at me all he likes. I flush it down the commode in dribs and drabs so nobody will see it and make a fuss. Same with the food. I carry it up a few cans at a time." She'd been smiling ever since she'd put her glasses on, but now she stiffened and her voice rose. "They want me out of here, you know. They've been trying to put me out for years. Me and my babies. I get threats, I get letters, and now I got another letter from this new owner just the other day, talking all this foolishness about health hazard and health inspectors. There's no health hazard. I keep it clean in here. You saw that."

I didn't say anything.

"I have no choice," she said. "It's hard. It's very hard, but I have to keep it clean or they'll get sick. I pray to the good Lord twenty times a day to give me strength and keep mine enemies from the gate. Now you better give that rascal to me before I open the door," she said. "Much as he loves you, I don't want him getting loose again."

I gave Fluffy one last kiss and handed him to the Cat Lady. She opened the door. "Iris," she called after me as I started down the stairs, "you tell your mama for me she's got a good daughter. You hear me? And you come up and visit anytime you want."

SO AFTER THAT, I STARTED RINGING HER BELL
when I finished walking Blackie. "Can I get you anything from downstairs?" I always asked. "Do you need
any help?" A lot of times she didn't answer, and other
times she just called, "No thank you, sugar," through
the door, but one time she said, "Buster's been asking
for you," and I came in and played with him in the living room while she read aloud from her Bible.

From then on, instead of saying, "Do you need
help?" I said, "Has Buster been asking for me?" and if
she opened the door, I'd come in and say hello to the
cats, and she'd ask how I was doing and tell me who'd
been mischievous that day, who'd beat up on whom,
who was feeling poorly. I never stayed more than a few
minutes. It was too hard on my nose.

"Do you play the piano?" she asked every time.

"No," I'd say.

"That's a shame," she always said. "I taught the piano for so many years. Children came from all over the neighborhood. Grown-ups, too. I still play at my church. Did I tell you that?" Sometimes she'd ask if I planned on going down to the bodega. I always said yes. She'd pull her change purse out of her big old pocketbook, unfold the bills, count out change, tell me why it wasn't good to feed tuna to cats, and decide if it was seafood supper she was running low on, lamb, or beefy dinner.

"So, Iris, you got your cat finally," Sammy said the first time I came to the cash register with three cans of cat food and a box of Cat Chow.

"It's not for me, it's for the Cat Lady," I told him.

"The Cat Lady? *Oye*, Junior!" he called over to where Junior was stamping prices. "You better watch out, or Iris'll be taking your job. She still giving those twenty-five cent tips?" he asked me. "Or is she paying you in piano lessons?"

"*Mira*, you think she gives them cats piano lessons?" Junior said. "I'm gonna ask her next time. I'm gonna ask if her cats play Mozart."

They made fun of her like that every time, laughing about her hats, her Bible quoting, how she paid with pennies—but then, when I gave Sammy her money, he'd go back to the shelf for a few more cans of cat food or another quart of milk, and tuck them in the bag. "It don't seem right for her to use up her whole check on them cats," he'd say. "Tell her there was a sale."

I'd earned enough money by then that each time I went down, I got myself some ice cream or a candy bar. When I knew Freddy was home, I'd get two. I wasn't totally doing it to soften him up so he'd take me to buy a bra, but it couldn't hurt.

I was getting big—up toward backpack-on-the-front big. Mami's gray bra with its six safety pins took care of the jiggling and bouncing, but I really did deserve better.

"Freddy, you know how stores like Price Rite sell, like, packs of panty hose and underpants?" I said, the Friday afternoon before Labor Day. I had thirty dollars by then, so I'd come home with a pint of mocha chip, his favorite. "You think they sell bras, too?"

"Now how would I know that?" he said.

"If they do sell them, that'd be perfect," I said, "because there's no one in those stores to say, 'May I help you.' Plus, there's one not that far from here." I served him some more ice cream. "So will you go there with me?"

He put his spoon down. "You already asked me that, and I said no. You think I'm like that pit bull? Feed me and I'll do anything you want?"

"No!" I tried to wipe the guilty look from my face. "Come on, Freddy, who else am I going to ask?"

"Ask one of your Bronx friends."

"They're away," I said. "I haven't talked to them since we moved." Besides, that felt like another life.

"Then ask Grandma. Ask Aunt Myra."

"And then Mami finds out I went behind her back?"

"What about one of your friends from the building?"

Yolanda? Her kids would have to come along. Luisa? I couldn't see it. Daisy would take me in a minute, but forget that. "I don't want to get into it with them," I said.

"So then I guess you're just gonna have to go by yourself," he said.

I must have had fifty dreams that night—one where I'd taken the subway to, like, New Jersey to buy a bra, and when I looked for my thirty dollars, I remembered I'd thrown it to Brutus and he'd eaten it, so I couldn't even get home; one where I was at school and kids were crowding around as if they liked me, till I looked down and saw that all I had on above the waist was two see-through butterfly wings; one where the Computer School was this giant computer and you couldn't get in without the password.

"But the only passwords I could think of were from

my typing book, like the lad had shad and the lass has gas," I told Will the next morning. I don't know how I got started on that. I'd never told him personal stuff before. "But then somehow I was inside and we were supposed to take a test, but I hadn't even gotten the book yet, and when I tried explaining that, the teacher was like, 'Dummy, this is the Computer School. There are no books. Why don't you know that? You've been here for a month—'"

I was sitting outside his window, and he'd been nodding, like maybe he'd had dreams like this, too, but now his face went all pinchy. "By the time I get to school, everyone *will* have been there for a month," he said.

"But your dad will get you down the stairs, won't he?" I said. "He has to, right? You have to get to school."

"You'd think."

My dreams suddenly seemed stupid and unimportant. "What'd you do last year? How *do* you get to school?" I hadn't thought about any of this.

"The bus. But first I have to get down to the bus. It comes way after my dad leaves for work."

Oh, God. "So then he'll have to leave later."

"I guess."

"Have you talked to him?"

"Sort of."

"Talk to him again."

"It won't help."

"What about trying to call the landlord? I know people wrote to the landlord about the elevator."

"Yeah, and has the landlord fixed it?"

"No, but your dad could write again. Or you could." I couldn't stand the way his eyes kept, like, blanking out on me. Why wasn't I getting through to him? "You can't just give up, Will. There's gotta be something you can do."

"Whatever." He pulled his peashooter from his pocket and loaded it with beans. "Now, would you mind moving over—"

"Yeah, shoot some pigeons," I said, getting to my feet. "That's really gonna help."

"Hey," he said, not looking at me. "It's not your problem."

Why did so many of our conversations end up with at least one of us mad? And why, when it was me, was it so hard to tell if I was madder at him or at myself? "Fine," I said. "I have my own problems."

That night, as soon as Mami went to bed, I knocked on Freddy's door. "Freddy," I said, "if I had other people to ask, I'd ask."

I could hear him in there, but he didn't answer.

"And I can't go by myself. I'm not allowed. I mean, what if I got run over by a bus? Mami'd kill me. She'd kill you, too, for not going with me."

That sounded lame, even to me. I opened his door. He was on his bed reading a magazine. "Freddy, d'you think about school at all?" I said. "Like what they'll think of you, and what it'll feel like, walking in the first day, not knowing anyone?"

"I know it'll feel a whole lot better without the Pinkowitz," he said, still reading. "No Pinkster, no Pinky—"

"What are you saying?" I grabbed the magazine away. "You're gonna change your name?"

"That's right. They ask me to fill out the forms the first day, I'm Frederick Diaz. Plain and simple."

Even as my mouth said, "You can't do that!" my mind was racing, thinking about no more "Pinkowitz? You don't look pink to me?" "What *are* you?" "Are you, like, adopted?" Being plain Iris Diaz would make life way simpler for me, too. I could be one thing, instead of neither one thing nor the other. And yet dropping the Pinkowitz would be like flushing half of me down the toilet—flushing Papi down the toilet. Maybe that's what Freddy wanted. . . .

But I couldn't think about that now.

"Freddy," I said before he could start reading again. "You told me something. Now can I tell you something?"

"Sure," he said. "'Long as it doesn't have to do with underwear."

"It does," I said. "Freddy, listen to me. I can't go by myself. I'm too scared."

"You expect me to buy that?" he said. "After the whole Just Ask Iris thing?"

I saw what he was saying, but it didn't change how I felt. "That's here," I said. "Inside the building. Outside is completely different."

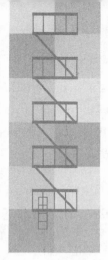

CHAPTER 17

BUT HE JUST WENT BACK TO READING, SO I COULD hardly believe it when the next morning he showed up in my room wearing his baseball cap, carrying his blue hooded sweatshirt.

"So we going or not?" he said.

"Going where?" I was afraid to hope.

"To Price Rite," he said. "Hey, I decided I could use some batteries."

I didn't tell him I hadn't had my breakfast. I didn't let myself throw my arms around him. I put my money in my pocket and we were out the door.

"So you're really gonna change your name?" I said as we headed to Broadway.

"I'm thinking about it," he said. "Don't say nothing to Mami, though. I don't know if it'll sit too well."

"Freddy, this is me you're talking to," I said. "You really think I'd tell Mami?"

"No, I know," he said. "I just don't want her going all ballistic on me before I even get it figured out."

"That's the story of my life," I said.

We'd been walking along like two normal people, but as soon as we hit Broadway, he put his Discman on and sped up so he was walking a few steps ahead of me. That was okay. He didn't have to talk to me, just come along. We headed downtown, past restaurants, bars, dry cleaners, convenience stores, till we reached the Price Rite. He waited by the batteries while I scouted around. I saw hair clips I would have liked having nail polish, tube socks, men's underwear, panty hose in every size and color. But no bras.

"They may have them at the next one," I said. We kept walking. The next one didn't have bras, either. Neither did Metro Health and Beauty Aids or the CVS. The sun bouncing off the sidewalk made it feel like we were walking across the Sahara Desert.

"You could try in here," Freddy said as we came to one of those bargain stores with the racks of house-dresses and bins of shoes and towels and big, old-lady underpants out on the sidewalk.

I made a face.

"If you see any better places, be my guest," he said. "But I'm not seeing any."

This store had some of everything—lace curtains hanging from the ceiling, picnic coolers, pillows, comforters, brooms, T-shirts—all so crammed together, a fat person would have to squeeze through the aisles. There had to be bras somewhere in there. But I did not want my first bra to be from some bin.

I was trying to decide if I needed one badly enough to go in when someone behind us called, "Yo, Pinky, man, whassup?"

Just from the way Freddy froze, I knew who it was. "Whatchu doin' here?" he said as Kevin came up beside us.

"Lookin' for you, man. And now I've found you." Kevin grinned at me. Or smirked. I could feel my face getting hot. I could see Freddy looking like he wanted to sink through the sidewalk. "Whatchu doin' here, buying your moms a new mop?"

"Nothin'," I said. "Just walking downtown."

"Yeah, just walkin' downtown," Freddy said.

"I'll walk with you," Kevin said, falling into step beside him.

I thought that was it for bra buying. Then, from a block away, I saw the Ninety-sixth Street bus crossing Broadway, getting ready to pull in to the bus stop. I grabbed Freddy's arm. "There's our bus!" I said. "The bus over to the East Side. If we run, we can get it!"

Would Freddy go for it? Or would Kevin ruin everything? We only had a second.

Freddy turned to him. He shrugged. "Hey. Sisters, man . . . you know how it is . . . catch you later!"

We got there just as the bus was about to close its doors.

"You owe me, Iris!" Freddy said as we sank into our seats. Thank God he had a Metrocard. "You owe me big-time!"

"I know!" I said. The air-conditioning felt so good. "But the East Side's better, anyway. You don't know anybody over there, right? And there'll be more stores."

There were, but they looked really snooty and expensive and none of them sold bras. Plus, everyone on the street was white and dressed nice, and I had on an old T-shirt and my flip-flops and cutoffs. We were here, though, so we kept walking. And walking. And walking—down Madison, over to Third Avenue, then down some more. Freddy must have been dying with that hot sweatshirt on.

We'd walked all the way to the Seventies without seeing anything when, across the street and down the block, I spotted Victoria's Secret. It was huge, and I could see the bras from here: animal prints, jungle prints, turquoise lace. I started walking faster. "Freddy, let's cross!"

When we got over there, I peered through the window. Snobby-looking salesgirls in black pantsuits were helping fancy ladies pick out silk underwear. A group of rich high school girls dressed like models leaned over a table stacked with bright-colored panties. "Look! That's exactly what I want!" I pointed at a table loaded with white bras. But it was the girls Freddy was looking at. He pulled his hood on. I grabbed his arm. "Come on!" I opened the door. Two cute high school boys looking at black shortie nightgowns stared out at us.

"Nooo, no, no!" Freddy broke free, tightened the drawstring on his hood to make it cover more of his face, and started across the avenue.

"Freddy, where you going?" I yelled after him.

"Hey, I came with you," he called over his shoulder. "I didn't say I'd go into a Victoria's Secret!"

To tell the truth, I was a little relieved not to go in there. But I didn't see anyplace else, and it was so hot. I caught up with him and we kept walking, past a movie theater, a flower store, shoe stores, a bunch of clothing stores. I could feel my face greasing up and the sweat running down my sides. My stomach was rumbling. Freddy'd taken his hood off, but he hadn't said a word to me in blocks.

I was starting to think maybe Mami's old gray bra wasn't that bad, that we should give it up and go home, when we came to a little store with a window full of old-lady flowered swimsuits and pink quilted bathrobes with matching slippers. I stopped walking.

"Lulu's Lingerie?" Freddy's eyebrow went up. "You're not serious. Iris, this is, like, where Grandma Lillian would buy her girdles."

"Then let's go back to Victoria's Secret." I was getting desperate.

"Fine. Then go in."

My stomach gave a lurch. "What if it's expensive?"

"Your thirty dollars is as good as anyone's," he said.

"What if they think I'm a shoplifter? What if they're mean? What if they call me 'little girl,' or if they only sell, like, Wonderbras, or triple D?" What if they made me take off all my clothes so they could inspect me to see what size?

"Hey, you're the one who wanted to go in," he said. "It's up to you."

The store was empty except for the lady with the blond perm and pink glasses. She seemed more like a school lunchroom lady than a snobby saleslady.

I went in.

"May I help you?" she said. I was sure she could hear my heart thumping.

"I . . . uh . . ." Oh, God. My voice sounded more like Fluffy's mewp than like someone who should be shopping on the East Side. "I . . . uh . . . need a bra."

"We specialize in brassieres," she said, "and foundation garments of every kind."

How red could a face get before you, like, had a stroke? "I don't know the size."

She smiled. "That shouldn't be a problem. I've been fitting girls like you for thirty-five years." She walked around to another counter. "Try these," she said, picking out four white ones. "They're cute and all quite moderately priced." She led me to a dressing room. I'd been terrified, when she'd said "fitting," that she'd come in with me, but she handed me the bras. "I'll be right here if you need anything," she said.

"Thanks." My hands fumbled as, one after another, I put them on. They all fit perfectly, and they were all cute. I was cute. This lady was a genius. I loved Lulu's Lingerie! But I could only afford one. How would I decide? I studied them. I tried them all again. Finally I picked the one with the tiny blue bow with the pearl in the center. Never again in life would I have to wear Mami's dingy gray bra!

"Thank you!" I told her as she wrapped the old bra in pink tissue paper and gave me my change. "Thank you so much."

I tried to thank Freddy, too, when I got outside with my little pink Lulu's Lingerie shopping bag, but when he saw me running toward him, he pulled his hood over his face. "Yo, Iris!" he said. "No kissing. Do not kiss me on the street!"

I could still see his eyes, though, and he looked almost as happy as I was.

"So I guess that's it for Just Ask Iris," he said as we started back uptown to catch the bus. He'd taken his sweatshirt off, finally. "It's Labor Day weekend. You got your bra. You can retire."

"Retire?" That was the last thing on my mind. Especially now, when I was feeling so good. "You can't start something called Just Ask Iris and then crap out on everyone," I said. "I've got customers who count on me." They weren't really customers. They were my friends. Even Will was my friend. Not to mention there were those other bras I could come back and buy as soon as I had some more money. "By the way, Freddy," I said, "I still have eleven dollars and five cents."

"Then since you're rich, and I'm starving," he said as we passed a hot-dog cart, "you can buy us a hot dog."

I bought him two. But even though I was starving, myself, I only got one, because I'd just had an excellent thought. I still had four of the hot dogs I'd bought for Brutus. I could get some rolls on the way home and take them up to Will's.

CHAPTER 18

I'D TOTALLY FORGOTTEN MOST PEOPLE DIDN'T work Saturdays.

"Hey, do I get some help with this, or what? This ain't all my mess, you know!" Will's dad, a dish towel on his shoulder, was washing dishes. "Will, get in here!" You wouldn't think a back could looked pissed off, but his did.

I'd just thrown Brutus my only two Milk-Bones. I edged away from Will's window onto the narrow part, praying Brutus wouldn't smell my hot dogs and start barking.

"I'll be right there, Dad," Will called. "I'm just get-ting my school stuff organized."

"Yeah, well, don't get too excited," his dad said as Will wheeled himself in. "I just asked the super again about the elevator, and it ain't looking good."

"So are you gonna call the landlord?" Will took a dish from the mountain on the drain board and started drying.

"I been calling. I called a half-dozen times." His dad cursed.

"What about calling the City, then? Or the Board of Education?" Will was standing up to him. He was doing what I said! "Or we could ask Uncle Rob. He helped us out that other time, remember? Dad, I think you should ask. If we call now, maybe he can work it out. It's only five more days to school."

"Look at me, Will!" His dad whirled around so fast, I was afraid he was going to hit him. "Do I look like I've forgotten that? You've been giving me the count-down for a month now! What happens the first day of school? Nothing. They're starting on a Thursday. What can happen? Nothing! You'll miss nothing!" I could imagine the spit flying out of his mouth every time he cursed.

And Will still wasn't backing down. "That's not true, Dad—"

"Not to mention it takes a month for the bus company to get their act together. Half the time I stand down there with you for twenty minutes and the bus don't even show up." He dropped his dish towel, stomped over to the fridge, and got himself a beer. "I never knew anyone with such a bug about school.

You'd think you'd be glad of an excuse not to go. Hey! Where you goin'? Will, come back here!"

I didn't realize till Will left the room that I'd been clutching the hot-dog rolls so tight, I'd squashed them flat. Not that it mattered now, I thought as I chucked them and the hot dogs to Brutus. I was the one who'd told Will to try talking to his dad. Had I made things worse? Would Will be even madder at me than he already was?

And what if Uncle Rob said no? No way could I carry Will down the steps. I doubted Freddy could, either. Mr. Gordon was too old. I didn't know Yolanda's husband, or Daisy's. Tattoo Man hated me, and Mr. Ocasio was not exactly the helpful type.

I thought all afternoon about asking Papi, but Mami was right. Even when Papi promised to help, you couldn't count on him. Will needed someone he could count on. As far as I could tell, the only one was me.

Worrying about it would have ruined my day if I hadn't been so happy with my bra. It was so much more comfortable than that thick, old, ugly gray thing and it made me look a thousand times better. I checked every time I went by the mirror. Of course, there *was* the small problem of telling Mami. I had no idea when that would happen. For now I put on a thick T-shirt and overalls shorts so she wouldn't notice.

I needn't have worried. The only thing she was looking at when she got home was her bed. "Stay with me, though," she said as she kicked off her shoes and lay down. "I'm not gonna sleep. You can sit right here with me and type. I've been working so many hours, I never get to see you anymore. I miss you, *m'ija*."

Which of course made me feel a little bad that I was lying to her about the bra.

Jujm jujm jujm jujm jujm hyjnm hiiuynm

Kik, kik, kik, kik, kik, kikk, kik ;ki;okkik ki;k

Aqaz swsx dedc frtv gtgb aqaz swsx
dedc frtv gtgb

The lad is tglassd. A sad lasd ha e a baad
dad/ Gladd was a bad dad!!!

At first I thought I'd quit as soon as she fell asleep. Which took about three minutes. But Will wasn't the only one worrying that it was five days till school.

Even if everyone at the Computer School was not a genius computer nerd, if I could barely type jujm kik . . .

If you woiuld nt be forgotten as sooon as you
are dead and rotten either write thihgdt
worth reasding or do things worth wriitng.

In the world of bussness,timidity avails nothing , nor sluggishenss notr laclkkof porpose...

Mr. Ellsworth Peabody, Esq.
Peabody, O"/holihoun & Wimtherrs
Broiokl6n, N. Y.

My dear Mr. Pepbdoy:
Too many compliant compalint letters   do nit
gove clearly the cause of the complaint. htyye
ramble onor exagggerate the injustive. THey
donot supply all the necetssay detals, or the
facts the reader requorws. . .

I was just telling myself what a saint I was for
sticking with it more than an hour when Freddy came
in from his room. "Yo, Iris, someone's knocking on
your ceiling."

"Uh-oh! Will!" I checked to make sure Mami was
still asleep. "If she wakes up, tell her I went to the
store. I'm going up."

I ran to the kitchen, grabbed some Milk-Bones,
rushed up the fire escape, and threw Brutus his biscuits.

"Hey!" Tattoo Man shoved the window up and
stuck his face at me. "What'd you just give my dog?"
He had pants on but no shirt, and, oh my God, he had a
million tattoos! Blue and red ones all over his chest.

I backed up as far as I could. Which was not far enough. "Nothing."

"No!" he said. "He just ate something. I saw him."

Brutus was whining for more. Tattoo Man grabbed his collar. "You better tell me what you gave him. And what are you staring at? You never saw a tattoo before?"

His eyes really did look like Dracula's. "It was just a Milk-Bone. A little one." That was a lie. It was a big one.

"Did anyone say you could feed my dog? Or step onto my fire escape? I told you I didn't want you up here. And how do I even know that was a dog biscuit? You know how much this dog cost me? You know how much it costs every time I have to take him to the vet, and you're throwing crap to him?"

"It wasn't crap!" Will called out his window. "It was a Milk-Bone. I gave them to her. And she's just coming to see me."

Thank God! I ran across to his window.

"This is supposed to be a watchdog," Tattoo Man hollered after me. "You keep this up, next thing you know, he'll be wagging his tail at all the burglars, saying, 'Yeah, just come on in. Sure, give me a Milk-Bone, you can take anything you want. Go ahead, rob me blind . . .'"

"You better come inside," Will said.

I peeked in the window. The kitchen was clean now, the dishes put away. "Where's your dad?"

"Out." He backed up the wheelchair so I could

climb in the window, but I stayed right by it in case I needed to leave quick. "He gets stir-crazy." He wheeled himself over to the cabinets. "You want some Frosted Flakes? He forgot to get the milk, but—"

"No, that's okay," I said. "You knocked?"

"Yeah." He nodded. "I just thought you should know . . . I don't kill pigeons."

This is why he wanted me to come up? "But . . . I thought . . ."

He made a face.

"Then why'd you say all that?"

"I don't know." He looked away and shrugged. "You know."

I was pretty sure I did know, so I nodded.

He shrugged again. "But you never know. I may nail one one some day."

I let that pass. "So is that what you wanted to tell me? That you're not the mighty pigeon killer?"

"No. I just wanted to clear that up." He nodded toward a chair. "You could sit if you want."

I sat on the radiator. "I was going to come by before with some hot dogs for us."

"Good thing you didn't," he said.

"Yeah," I said.

"I tried talking to him," he said.

Did you call Uncle Rob, I wanted to ask? Did you work it out? "How'd it go?" I said.

"It didn't. Big surprise."

"Will!" A yell came from the front of the apartment. "I'm home!"

I jumped up, climbed out the window, and edged over to the side. Will followed me to the window. I knew I should get out of there, but his dad didn't seem to be coming in, and I couldn't leave it. "Will, you know, there's always Tattoo Man," I said. "We could ask him to help."

Will snorted. "He hates my dad worse than he hates you."

"Then we'll find someone else," I said. "Will, we'll figure something out."

"What's this 'we'?" he said. "I told you before. It's not your problem."

He started to turn away, but when I said, "So are you telling me to mind my business?" he turned back and shook his head.

"No," he said.

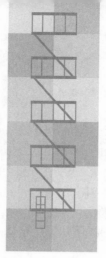

CHAPTER 19

I DIDN'T THINK I'D SEE WILL, OR ANYONE ELSE in the building, till Labor Day was over and Mami went back to work, but at 6:30 Monday morning, he knocked again. Mami always slept in on holidays, but I tiptoed through Freddy's room and peeked in the living room to make sure. Then, praying Tattoo Man was sleeping in, too, I went back to my room, threw my clothes on, grabbed some biscuits, and went out the window.

Whew. No Brutus or Tattoo Man. That was a relief.

"What are you doing up so early?" I asked Will when I got to his landing.

"I'm always up early," he said. "I was just thinking. When we were talking about school before? I don't know what grade you're in. I don't even know your last name."

"Pinkowitz," I said. "Now you're gonna laugh, right?"

"Hey"—he nodded toward his legs—"do I look like somebody who's about to laugh at people's names?"

I sat down on the step. "My brother's going to change his," I said. "To my mom's name, Diaz."

He frowned. "Did I even know you had a brother?"

"I know." I nodded. "You need to get out more."

He snorted and nodded at the same time. "And he wants to change it because of the whole half-and-half thing, or 'cause he hates your dad?"

How did he know? "Probably both. We didn't really get into it. I don't know yet what I think."

He was still nodding. "I can relate. So how old is this brother? What grade *are* you in?"

"He's fourteen," I said. "And I'm in seventh. You?"

"Eighth."

That's what I'd thought. "So what school you go to?" I hoped he'd say Computer.

"Endeavors, down by Lincoln Center. It's the only middle school in Manhattan that can handle wheelchairs. That's not where you're going, by any chance?"

"No." I shook my head. "I'm going to Computer. Why, I can't tell you, since I know zero about computers except that I hate typing—"

"I heard Computer was okay," he said. "I was supposed to go to Hunter. You've heard of that, right? It's a great school. I mean, I passed the entrance exam and everything, but then"—he started picking at his finger-nails—"you know, with the accident and the rehab, and then it turned out they couldn't deal with the chair. Something about the right lockers, or enough room in the bathrooms. . . . Now I heard they worked it out, except now it's too late because you can only start there in the seventh grade."

"Will, that's so terrible!" I said.

"Nah. It's okay. Endeavors isn't bad. I like it. And I might go to Stuyvesant next year. Or Bronx Science. I know I can pass the test—"

He was talking about the hardest schools in New York City. "You must be really smart."

"No smarter than you," he said. "You could get into those places."

"I suck at school," I said.

He looked up. "Why? You seem like the type who always has her hand in the air." He shot his hand up and started waving it and calling in a high voice, "Ooh, ooh, teacher, teacher, over here! Yo, yo, teacher, I got it!"

"Uh-uh. No." I shook my head. "That's not me. I don't think I raised my hand once all of last year."

"You expect me to believe that?" he said. "You got something to say about everything."

"Not in class," I said. "In class I either blank out or else something stupid comes out. I can just hear myself." I put on my Mildred voice:"'All right, Iris, tell the class the formula for the circumference of a circle,' and I'm like, 'In the world of business, timidity avails nothing, nor sluggishness nor lack of purpose. The quizzical jumping chef speedily provided an extra dozen ducks. As early as the fifth century B.C., parchment was made from the skins of sheep and goats.'" Will had started laughing, so I kept going. "'In the small cities of South America one does not have to send to the store for a container of milk. The concise complaint letter avoids unnecessary introductions and wordy endings. Major experimental quandaries have confronted quiz wizards—'"

"You're crazy, you know that?" he said.

"You think I make this up," I said. "It's straight out of my typing book."

"And you remember it?"

"That's what I've been doing this whole weekend," I said. "Sitting with my mom, typing. It's not like I try to remember. It just happens."

"As I was saying," he said, "you're smart."

"Right." I tried not to show how pleased I was. "I'm picking up all kinds of valuable information, but I still can't type."

"Oh, yeah?" he said. "Let's see you type."

"Now?" I said. "At six-thirty in the morning?"

"You doing anything else?" he said.

"No, but why would anyone want to see me type?"

He shrugged.

"I mean, unless you feel like falling down laughing—"

"Maybe I do."

"What about your dad?"

He made loud snoring noises. "If you want, I'll go check." He left, then came back. "Yeah, he's out. Dead to the world. So what do you think?"

"It means going past Tattoo Man's house again and sneaking into my mom's room for the typing book," I said.

"Forget Tattoo Man," Will said. "He was up partying till three last night. I heard him. He won't be awake. Don't worry."

So I ran down, grabbed the typing book without Mami even stirring, and ran back up.

Will's computer looked a lot newer than ours, with a bigger screen and a printer.

"This is nice," I whispered. I looked at his closed door. "But isn't your dad sleeping in the next room?"

"Nah. He conked out in the living room last night and he's still there. As much beer as he had, he won't be moving for a while. And I closed both doors." He nodded toward the computer. "Sit down. Try it."

Hmm. . . . Would using both my names be better or worse?

"Here, let's make it bigger." Will moved over next to me, and did something with the mouse that made the letters on the screen twice as big.

I typed his name. WILL GLADD. "Do you have, like, Email and the Internet?"

He nodded.

I typed WILL GLADD HAD A SHAD. "I don't have any of that stuff. My computer is so old . . ."

He picked up Mildred and started flipping through it. "Yeah, are you sure you're not going to the Type-writer School?"

"That's exactly what I keep telling my mom!" I typed ALAS A LASS'S GLASSES

"On the other hand," he said, "they're gonna make you type papers, so you do need to know how to type."

"Hey, whose side are you on here?" A LASS'S ASS'S GASSY BASS

"Yours." He flipped more pages. "Okay. You ready? Type, 'Dear Doris.'"

DRER DPROIS, I typed.

"I see what you mean," he said. "You're not too good."

"It's because you're sitting here!" I said. "You're making me too nervous."

"Okay." He backed away. "Now, type, 'Helen and I enjoyed every minute of our delightful visit—'"

THE DAD OF GLADD HAD A GASSY BASS. "Go to the complaint letters," I said. "They're funnier."

He turned pages. "Look, here's that thing you were saying before. 'The concise complaint letter avoids unnecessary introductions and wordy endings. It leaves the reader with no doubt what he must do—'"

"I told you I didn't make it up," I said.

He flipped more pages. "Here we go. Let's see if you can type this without any mistakes." He read very slowly: "'Dear Sir or Madam: I am writing to complain in the strongest possible terms about the ironing board cover my wife purchased on 4 December.'" He waited for me to stop typing. "'She has called your establishment on numerous occasions . . .' Do you need me to spell that?"

"That's okay," I said, trying not to crack myself up as I typed.

"What's so funny?" He came closer and read aloud over my shoulder: "'I am writiging to complain in the strognsest possible terms aoubt the jumping chef. The extra dozen ducks did not arrive speedily. They were dead.' Uh, Iris?" He was cracking up, too. "That's not what I told you to type."

"But it leaves the reader with no doubt what he must do, right?"

"Yeah. Send new ducks," he said.

"This could be why I don't type better," I said. "Because who cares about Doris and her ironing board? I mean, if that's all they can think of to complain about

. . . and why is the husband writing her letter for her? Listen, if I was typing my own letter? About something I cared about? I'm sure I could do a perfectly good typing job—"

Will was nodding. "Me, too. Just, the complaint letter I'd write wouldn't do any good. Dear Sir or Madam. I live at 532 West 109th Street, Apartment 3B. The elevator has been broken for six weeks. My father has called the landlord at least once a week—"

"You want me to type that?" I said. "Because I will."

"For what?" He looked so bitter suddenly. "Whenever you call, they always promise they'll do something, but they never do . . ."

I couldn't tell if he was talking to me or going on with his complaint letter, but I started typing what he was saying. I couldn't stop to figure out how to do a new paragraph, so I added it to the duck stuff, typing as fast as I could.

". . . There are old people in this building and babies in strollers, not to mention that I myself am in a wheelchair. School starts this week, and without an elevator there's no way—"

"Will, slow down!" I was making a million mistakes. "I can't type, remember?"

"Nobody told you to type this," he said. "I'm just saying what I'd put if it was me writing the complaint letter and not stupid Doris."

But he kept rattling it off, so I kept trying to get it down. I'd written at least ten more lines when a shout came from the other room.

"Yo, Will! Rise and shine! 'The best part of waking up is Folgers in your cup.'"

I practically knocked the chair over in my rush to get out.

"Oops!" Will whispered as he followed me to the kitchen. "I forgot to make his coffee. I'm making it now, Dad!" he yelled back as I headed for the window.

"This was fun," he said as I scrambled out. "In a depressing kind of way. I'll save the letter if you want. For our next typing practice."

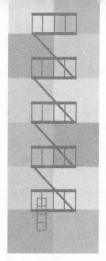

CHAPTER 20

"EXCUSE ME, MISS," I SAID. "COULD I GET BY YOU, please?" The lady talking to Mr. Ocasio on the stoop was blocking my way out the door. It was Tuesday morning. Mami'd gone to work. I'd walked Blackie, but I'd forgotten to mail Luisa's phone bill, so I'd come down again.

The lady moved her briefcase just enough for me to get past. What was she doing here, with that alligator briefcase, and that suit that looked like it cost a thousand dollars, and those long red nails, and those four-inch heels? I couldn't decide if she looked beautiful or mean, or both. Her legs were skinnier than mine, but I loved the shoes. Her cell phone rang. "Whaaat! Yeah. 532. Yeah. I'm there now. Yeah. Not good!" She had a loud, mean voice.

She had to be from some welfare agency or from

the landlord. The way Mr. Ocasio was slumped down—
like a kid caught smoking in the boys' room—she was
probably from the landlord. Which meant she *could* be
here about the elevator.

She was still talking when I got back from the mailbox. I pretended to be reading the signs on the bodega
window: MILK $1.69 A GALLON. CAFÉ EL PICO 10 OZ. CAN
$2.99. *PRODUCTOS MEXICANOS.* She reminded me of some-
body. Somebody famous.

"Yeah, no, I agree with you," she said into the phone.
"There's nothing to decide. It's gone on way too long."

It had to be the elevator. And about time. It was
just two days till school.

"Hector!" She hung up and turned back to Mr.
Ocasio. "Did you even talk to her? I told you to talk to
her." Mr. Ocasio didn't answer.

Uh-oh. She'd caught me staring. "Do you live in
this building? What's your name?" she demanded, as
if she were my teacher, or the principal, or the truant
officer.

Now I knew who she reminded me of! Cruella De
Vil, the evil lady in *101 Dalmatians.* No wonder Mr.
Ocasio didn't want to answer her.

Luckily, she seemed to have forgotten me. "Listen
to me, Hector! I don't want to find you sitting in your
apartment when I get back. Not if all that mess in the
basement isn't cleaned up." She checked her watch,
then walked over to the black car by the curb. "And you'd

better get cracking," she warned as she unlocked the door. "Because I'll be back to check right after lunch. And I'll want you to go up there with me."

"I don't need this!" he started muttering as soon as she drove away. "The old owners, if they wanted me to do something, all they had to do was ask me and I did it. This lady, she's all over me as if it's my fault . . ."

I stopped even pretending to be reading signs. "But she's going to fix the elevator, right?"

"You think I know?" He shook his head. "That lady is a big headache to me, let me tell you, Iris."

"She's scary," I said.

"I'm talking about 6B," he said. "6B's causing me all kinds of trouble."

What? 6B was the Cat Lady! "What's up?"

"Same as the last time," he said. "Another flood."

I didn't get it. "Flood? What does that have to do with 6B?"

"I keep telling her what happens when you dump that cat litter in the toilet bowl," he said. "It goes straight down to the basement, and it hardens in the pipes just like cement. Next thing I know, I got eighteen inches of water in the basement, the elevator shaft's full of water, and this is not clean water we're talking, the motor burns out . . ."

Was he saying the problems with the elevator were the Cat Lady's fault?

"She's telling me I didn't tell 6B," he said. "I told her. I told her the last time it happened, right after the building changed hands. I told her till I was blue in the face. I keep telling her. But she don't want to listen, and now eleven other tenants got to pay the penalty—"

"What penalty? What are you talking about?" I said.

"Why do you think the new owner don't want to fix the elevator?" he said. "Why do you think it stays broken?"

He had to be really upset to be telling *me* this. "You mean all the Cat Lady's talk about the health inspector, and that letter from the landlord Luisa wanted me to translate? That's what it was about? Plumbing?"

"Yeah. Plumbing. And I don't know what to say to any of 'em, not the tenants, not the office . . ." He looked at his watch. "I gotta get down there. She's saying she'll be back after lunch. I don't get that stinkin' mess cleaned up, it's not just my job I lose, it's the apartment, too."

I felt like *I'd* just swallowed a load of cement. "What's she gonna do?"

"You heard her. She'll go up to 6B and look around. Depending on what she finds, she'll call the City. And they'll come get the cats. And then—"

"They can take away her cats?" I suddenly remembered the stuff in the landlord letter about tenants violating their leases by having pets. "Can they do that?"

"They could do anything they want!"

Take Fluffy? And those cute kittens, and those old, rickety cats? It would scare Jitters to death. Not to mention the Cat Lady! "What if she won't let them in?" I said.

"Then," he said, "it could get ugly. It could get ugly, anyway. There's nothing they'd like better than to get that old woman out and jack up the rent. I don't know." He shook his head again. "Maybe it had to happen sooner or later. *Una vieja loca* like that, no family to look out for her, it's no good to be living up there all alone. *Puede que todo sea para bien—*"

"They're not going to evict her?" I said. "They wouldn't do that, right?" How could that be for the best?

"This new management?" he said. "I don't put nothing past them."

If only we could put the cats in my house! But there was no way.

I wished Freddy was home, but he wasn't. Without even bothering with dog biscuits for Brutus, I ran up the fire escape and told Will what was going on.

"She's like Cruella De Vil!" I told him. "Even Mr. Ocasio's scared of her. And she'll be back here in a few hours. I don't know what to do. I don't even know how many cats the Cat Lady's got up there. It could be hundreds. And it stinks in there. If Cruella walks in and smells it . . . we've got to get the litter out. It's proof she's guilty. It's evidence. They'll evict her. They're already trying. Did you see that letter from the landlord about unsanitary conditions, health code violations?" My thoughts were coming so fast, I was tripping on my words. "Will, you have to help me!"

"Me?" Will raised his hands. "I'm afraid you've got the wrong guy."

"Yeah, well, I don't exactly have a dad, right? And my brother's not home—"

"Iris, hello?" he said. "See this wheelchair? I'm a cripple, remember. I can't walk."

"I know that." I felt panic rising in my throat. "But this is an emergency! Will, I need you."

"To do what?" he said. "Suck up sewage with a straw? Open your eyes, Iris. Do I look like somebody who can help anyone with anything? I'm useless."

I was so mad now, my eyes were blurring. "Why can't you just say you'll help me?" I shouted. He wouldn't look at me. "I could see if you're upset with the Cat Lady, because maybe it's her fault we have no elevator. But I'm asking you to help me, and you're saying you won't even try? You're gonna sit here whining, feeling sorry for yourself, when I've just finishing telling you I need you?" No way was I going to cry in front of him. I turned to go up the stairs. "It's not your legs that's the problem," I said. "You're right. Forget you. I'll get somebody else."

Except there was nobody else.

"So then what are you gonna do?" Will said.

I'd already started up the fire escape. "What do you care? You're useless, remember? I'm going up to talk to her."

"And say what?"

"I don't know." I couldn't look at him. "I'll think of something!"

"Yo, Iris, wait." He reached out the window and touched my leg. "Hold up a minute."

I stopped.

"If you go up there shaking like that, it won't work. You can't go up without a plan. It'd be like when you fell in her window and she got all crazy."

"What are you saying?" I stepped back down onto his landing.

"We'll put Fluffy here," he said.

"Your dad won't like that."

"My dad's not back till four-thirty. We can probably put some more cats in here, too, at least till then, if you can get 'em down here. Worst case, we'll stick 'em in my closet." He cursed and slammed his fist against his leg. "If only that elevator wasn't broken!"

"What?" I glared at him. "You gonna start whining again?"

"No!" he said. "But if we had the elevator, I could go down to the bodega for some boxes to carry the cats down here. That way they could definitely go in the closet. And we could put food and water in there for them—"

"I can do that," I said. "I could run down there now—"

"I thought you were going up to see the Cat Lady."

"That's right!" I looked at my watch. Nine-fifteen. "What're you doing?" I said as he pulled out his pen and grabbed my hand.

"Giving you my number," he said, writing on my palm. "As soon as you get up there, give me hers." He pulled a phone from a pouch thing on the side of the wheelchair. "I'll keep watch at the front window and I'll call Sammy about the boxes. When do you think this lady's gonna come?"

"After lunch," I said.

"What time is that?"

"We don't know."

"What about Ocasio?" he said. "Is he on our side?"

I started to say *our*, excuse me? But I changed my mind.

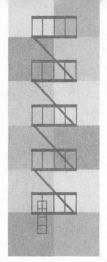

CHAPTER 21

THE CAT LADY'S HOUSE SMELLED EVEN WORSE today.

"I knew this day was coming!" she said as she pulled me inside. "I've been waiting for this day. Help me, Iris! Help me push this bureau in front of the door!" She leaned her weight against it. A black cat jumped off and ran into the bedroom.

"Stop, please! You'll hurt yourself!" I begged. There were cats everywhere. My insides, which had quieted down when Will started to help, were all in knots again.

She kept pushing. "'I will not be afraid, though they have set themselves against me. Save me, my God, for thou hast smitten mine enemies upon the cheekbone. Thou hast broken the teeth of the ungodly.'" Her face got redder and redder, but the bureau was not moving. "Iris, come over here and push!"

I was scared she'd give herself a heart attack. "This isn't what we should be doing," I said. "Please, we need to make a plan—"

"'The foolish shall not stand in thy sight. Thou hatest all workers of iniquity. Thou shalt destroy landlords and those that speak of leasing!' Pray with me, Iris! We can't let them take my babies!"

I didn't know any prayers. Nobody in my family prayed except my grandmas, and one of them prayed in Hebrew.

"Pray, Iris!" She was puffing and panting. "Push and pray!"

It wasn't a prayer, but it was all I could think of: "'In the world of business, timidity avails nothing, nor sluggishness, nor lack of purpose . . . *Oooof!*'" I leaned my full weight against the chest and pushed. It didn't budge. "We can't keep them out," I told her. "It's their building. If they want to come in, they'll get in. And if they don't—"

"'But those who look upon the Lord will renew their strength.'" Her voice rose higher. "'They will mount up with wings like eagles, they shall run and not grow weary, they shall walk and not grow faint—'"

"'If you would not be forgotten when you're lying dead and rotten . . . *Oooof!*'" I pushed again. "They're not going to do anything to you when they come in, okay?" I hoped to God I wasn't lying. "Really. They just want to take a look around."

That chest was not going anywhere.

We couldn't move the bookcase, either.

The Cat Lady sank onto her sofa, pulled a lace hankie from her sleeve, and wiped her forehead. A yellow cat and a gray one jumped up and pushed their noses in her face. "Oh, Peanuts, Maybelle, what am I going to do?" She sighed. "She's telling me the landlord just wants to come in and look around. That's what they all say. And then next thing you know, they'll be back here with a big sack, throwing all of you in it—"

"No!" I said. "That's why we have to get ready for them! We'll work it out—"

"They'll work it out all right." She was still talking to the cats. "They'll work us right out onto the street. That's what they want—"

Calm down, Iris, I told myself. If you calm down, maybe she will, too. "That's why we have a plan," I said.

I reached for the phone and dialed Will's number. He picked up on the first ring.

"No sign of them," he said. "I'm staying by the window. And I told Sammy I needed boxes and he's gonna send Junior up with a few. Plus I found a bunch more boxes in the closet. Iris, I think we can pull this off. How you're doin' on your end?"

"Okay." If only he could come up here and help me deal with this! "I guess."

"Great. How's the Cat Lady?"

I looked at her sitting there clutching her cats, her lips moving in a prayer. "Okay." Please don't go crazy on me, I begged her silently. "Just call when the boxes get there, all right, Will, and I'll come right down. And Will, call if anything happens." I gave him the number. "That was Will," I told her. "Will Gladd. From downstairs? Will's our lookout. He'll call when the manager comes. See, we do have a plan." I tried hard to smile.

She nodded, but she was looking more and more rattled. I could see panic in her eyes.

"Okay," I said. "Now, while we're waiting for Will to get the boxes together, no disrespect, okay, but we gotta do something about the smell."

"It smells in here?" She looked horrified. "I don't smell anything." She sniffed, sniffed again. "You see, I have to keep these windows closed. I don't dare open them—"

"I know," I said, "but now we have to open them. We'll open all the windows, then we're going to take out those bags of dirty litter, and then we'll find places for—"

"I'm going to have to explain to my babies what you're doing so they won't jump up on the sill and fall out," she said.

"They won't fall out. I told you. We're going to find good places for them."

Why hadn't Will called yet about the boxes?

Her eyes darted around the room. "What places? I have to talk to them. I don't know if they'll agree . . ."

How was she going to know if they agreed? Why was she arguing with me? How did you argue back to a crazy person? I was way, way over my head.

I called Will. "Will," I whispered. "It's not going well up here. This isn't going to work."

"Why not?" he said. "It's going really well on my end. Junior just brought up a bunch of boxes, and I called up Luisa Serrano and she gave me Yolanda's number and Daisy's, and I just called them, and they said they could take some cats—"

I'd never heard him like this. Will was pumped.

"That's great, Will," I said. "That's fantastic. But"— I looked at the Cat Lady, who had stood up and was going, "*Pssss!* Here, kit, kit, kit!" in a quivery, quavery voice—"we've got a real problem here. I've got some real questions about this."

"What?" he said. "This was your idea—"

"I know"—I dropped my voice still more—"and I know we can't just let the landlord come in and see this and put her out, but . . ."

Cats were running into the living room with us. More stood in the doorway trying to decide whether to come in. Others ran in from the kitchen. And the Cat Lady was still calling, "Come here, babies! Come on!" I recognized Ronald and Hyacinth and Thomas Jeffer-

son. "*Pssss, pssss!* That's right, everyone. Come on in."
In walked Sweet William, Dolly, Fast Eddie, Eleanor,
Bo Peep, plus cats I'd never seen before, at least thirty
of them, maybe more. Fluffy came over and rubbed
against my leg.

"I don't know, Will. Mr. Ocasio was saying before
that maybe it's too much for her, up here by herself
with all these cats—"

"Iris, you're not wimping out on me?" Will sounded
really upset. "You got this started. And now I've got all
these people in the building psyched—"

"I know that, but—"

"You babies have to understand," she was telling
the cats. "These people who want to take all of you
away? They think they know me. They don't know me.
They don't know the first thing about me. All they know
is I'm black and I'm old and I'm poor. They think my
first name is Cat and my last name is Lady and that I've
lost my marbles . . ."

"Will, hang on a second." I turned to her. "Ms.
Witherspoon. Your name's Ms. Witherspoon."

"Ms. Margaret Witherspoon." She nodded. "See,
babies, at least there's one person who knows." Her
voice had stopped wobbling. "Now all of you listen
to me."

"Iris," Will said, "you still there?"

"Just a sec," I said.

She stood up straighter. "The day I've been warning you about has arrived," she told the cats. "But we're not alone. We've got a young friend here to help us. Now we've got to pull ourselves together. Do you think you can do that?"

"Will," I said, "something's happening! I've gotta go."

"What? What are you gonna do? You gonna come and get the boxes or not?"

"I don't know yet." I set the phone down. "Ms. Witherspoon—"

"They're waiting for you, Iris," she said. "You're going to have to explain everything to them. Stand up tall, so they'll know you're making a speech. And speak slowly. Not everybody will understand. Some of them are brighter than others. But they'll all listen respectfully, isn't that right, Sweet William?"

The cats weren't listening. They were doing what cats always do—sitting, standing, perching, scratching, sniffing, licking themselves, walking around.

"Will," I said, "I'll call you back."

I cleared my throat and faced the cats. "Okay . . . everybody . . ." This was stupid. Beyond stupid. But at least the Cat Lady—Ms. Witherspoon—was listening. "This afternoon you're going on a little trip," I said. "There are a lot of very nice people in this building who will take good care of you. They all really like . . ."

Did I have to call them babies, or was I allowed to say the word "cat" in front of them? I looked over at her. Better not. ". . . and you'll all have to stay in . . . in . . ." I didn't want to say boxes, either. ". . . little . . . cardboard houses. But it's just for a few hours, okay, and we'll make sure you have food and water. And then when Cru . . . the manager lady's gone, we'll bring you all back up here, and everything will be fine." Ms. Witherspoon was nodding as I talked. "Okay," I said. "Is that cool with all of you?"

I turned to Ms. Witherspoon, trying not to look as stupid as I felt. "How was that?" I said.

"Very good," she said. "But you don't need to talk to them in that high, squeaky voice. You can talk to them normally. That's what I try to do. Iris"—she took me by the arm and led me to the corner—"let me tell you something. I talk to them like they're my children and I treat them like my children, but when you get right down to it, they're cats, and you know it and I know it, and those people who want to take them away from me most certainly know it. And the Lord helps those who help themselves. . . ."

I almost cried with relief.

"I've got to call Will back," I said.

"That's right," she said. "Call your friend back. Then we'll do what we have to do."

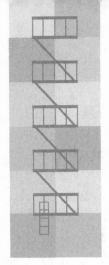

CHAPTER 22

"YOU GOT THE LITTER MOVED?" WILL SAID.

"Not yet." He'd been calling every couple of minutes. I clamped the phone between my ear and shoulder so I could keep loading litter boxes into Ms. Witherspoon's old red wagon so we could haul them to the fire escape. Thank God she had a long phone cord. "At least we've got the bags out of the tub and onto the fire escape."

"Good. I checked my closets," he said. "We can fit Fluffy and at least two more cats, maybe three—"

"I don't want to be around when Mr. Gordon looks out his window!" I said. "I had to shove the bags onto his side so I can get down the stairs." I'd sweated through my shirt wrestling with those bags. My glasses were so greased up, I could hardly see, and I hated to think what my hands smelled like, but I didn't dare stop to wash them. "You better pray we can fit these litter boxes out there, too!"

"We'll make them fit," Ms. Witherspoon said, adding another pan onto the two-foot stack already in the wagon. "We are bound and determined."

"How's she doing?" Will lowered his voice. "Is she freaking out?"

"Not so far." I was the one jumping each time I heard a noise, imagining the landlord tossing her stuff out on the street and guys with nets coming for the cats. And I didn't dare let her know. Not when she was working so hard here, doing so well, telling the cats, "We're going to hold it together. That's right. Because we've got this nice girl helping us now, God bless her heart."

"Wait'll you see what I did with the boxes," Will said. "Yo, we're talking cat hotels here, luxury cat accommodations—"

"How many do you have?" I said.

"So far, eight."

"Eight? Will, I'm looking at at least fifteen cats right here in the kitchen." I still didn't know how many there were in all. Ms. Witherspoon wouldn't let me herd them into one room so I could count them.

"Eight, uh-uh! We need more than eight," Ms. Witherspoon chimed in. "Tell him eight won't even make a dent."

"I know!" Will said. "That's why I called Lorna, over

at the grocery store. She says they've got plenty of boxes. We just have to get them over here."

"How?" I didn't bother asking who Lorna was or what grocery store. "I'm up to my eyeballs here. There's no way I can get boxes!" My nose was about to fall off from the ammonia stink. "Will, you got any air freshener down there? Lysol, room deodorant, anything?"

"Incense," he said. "My dad's got some incense. No, wait. I know. My mom's perfume!"

That had to be precious to him. I couldn't believe he was offering me that. "No, Will," I said. "We're not taking your mom's perfume."

"Hold on. Just a minute." Ms. Witherspoon hurried to her bedroom and came back with a tray of perfume bottles. "And if we use these up, I've got more." She set the tray down and began spraying. "Gardenia," she said as a sickly sweet smell filled the air. "From the Gadsden girl. They all gave me presents, all my piano students, every Christmas." She walked around the kitchen, spraying. "Cologne or handkerchiefs, every year. I told these cats I was holding on to that cologne for something. This must have been why." She sprayed another bottle. "Hmmm. Evening in Paris. That was from Mrs. Brown's boy." And another. "Freesia. My word, that's powerful."

Yes, but the combination of cat piss and flowers was not a good one. And Will was still talking about boxes, and Ms. Witherspoon was listing piano students and their mothers, and it was twenty after eleven and the house still stank, and she wouldn't let me open any windows till the cats were out, but I couldn't get the cats out without the boxes and even when we had the boxes, I still had to stuff the cats into the boxes, get them down to the neighbors . . . *Yaaahhh!* I need more time! I felt like screaming.

Then it came to me. We had no time. But I still had some money, and if I got jobs the rest of today and tomorrow . . .

I stopped loading litter boxes. "Ms. Witherspoon, put your cologne away! Will, call Sammy and get Junior to bring us air freshener. As much as we can buy for seven dollars. And see if Junior can go get Lorna's boxes. Tell him I owe him big-time. But he has to hurry. And Will, if you put your eight boxes by your window, I'll get them in a minute."

"Go now," said Ms. Witherspoon. "I'll take care of the litter."

I ran down the fire escape to my apartment, grabbed my money and, ignoring Brutus yelping for his biscuit, ran back up to Will's.

He was waiting for me at the window.

"Junior'll do it!" he said. "He's taking the bike over to the store. Sammy's picking out the deodorizers. I told him to bring everything to me because we don't want anyone to see him carrying boxes to Ms. Witherspoon's. Was that right?"

"Perfect!" I handed the money through the window.

"Now look at this." He reached down and picked up a big Pampers box. "Ta-da! The Fluffy Sheraton."

He'd cut a window in one side of the box and stapled cardboard strips across it like bars, so a cat couldn't climb through.

"Oh, my God, Will!" This was wonderful.

"And look here"—his eyes were shining as he tilted the box so I could see inside—"it's got a towel to sit on, so he'll be nice and comfortable, a bowl for food and a bowl for water"—I recognized his dog's dishes in the bottom—"and see"—he held out a roll of packing tape—"if you need to, you can tape the top shut so he can't jump out. I told Junior to only get boxes with tops so we can tape them closed." He checked his watch. "Uh-oh. Back to my lookout post. I'm not letting Cruella slip by me. I'll leave all the boxes here for you. The air spray, too."

If I hadn't been out the window, I'd have thrown my arms around him.

I carried Fluffy's box and two others up with me. "This is going to work!" I told Ms. Witherspoon as she and I began boxing cats. "I can feel it. It's going to be okay!"

Sure enough, Fluffy came when I called, and when

Ms. Witherspoon put a blob of cat food in the bowl, he jumped right in his box. And even though he looked worried when I closed him in, I got him to Will's with no trouble.

Up and down the fire escape I went. Miss Lucy and Bo Peep were easy, too. So was Big Boy. And by the time we'd stashed all four of them in their boxes in Will's closets, Junior had delivered the air freshener and started bringing Will more boxes.

Up and down I went, carrying up boxes, delivering cats, while Ms. Witherspoon put the last of the litter boxes out the window, plugged in the Plug-Ins, lit the scented candles, sprayed the entire house with air freshener, and then sprayed it again. Sammy'd given us a whole lot of air freshener for seven dollars!

It was past noon now, too late for Will to do anything fancy with the boxes—he didn't dare leave his lookout post—but Ms. Witherspoon put a can of cat food and a margarine container bowl in every one. "They don't like eating out of the can," she said.

A few cats were curious enough to jump right in their boxes. Most weren't that easy.

"Now you know why I call him Fast Eddie," Ms. Witherspoon said as a striped cat shot under the refrigerator. "Careful of Hyacinth! She bites!" she warned as a fat white cat left tooth marks in my thumb. "You'll never catch Heckle and Jekyll. You can probably catch

Jitters, but it'll give her a nervous breakdown if we try to move her. And you don't want to take the obstreperous ones." She named a whole bunch of other cats it was best to leave. But one way or another we tricked, shoved, bribed, and dumped a lot of cats into a lot of boxes. It was a good thing I had so much tape.

Up and down. Up and down. Yolanda'd said she'd take two cats, but not to help the Cat Lady. "Me, I'd just as soon they got her out," she said. "I'm doing it for you." I pretended I thought she meant two boxes and brought her four. "You'd better bring them around front, though," she said when I showed up at her window with Minnie and Mickey. "You don't want to get Cuca started. It's bad enough he thinks he's a telephone and an ambulance." So I brought the box back up the fire escape and back down the stairs.

I brought Luisa six cats. She said she could take more if we needed her to.

Have you ever tried going down a fire escape carrying a big, bulky box with a ten-pound cat inside it, jumping around, howling like he's being murdered? My legs were killing me. My arms ached. I was totally scratched up from cats trying to climb out before we could tape them in. I was hungry. I was thirsty. Every time I got another box from Will's, Brutus barked and carried on. But Will kept calling to report that there was no sign of the manager lady, and every cat I moved was one less cat in the apartment, so I ignored all of it and kept going.

Daisy tried to change her mind on me, saying she didn't need any nasty cats messing up her clean house, until I reminded her that she hated the landlord even more than she hated cats. Then, instead of big old ugly cats, I brought her kittens.

"*Mira, qué preciosa!*" she cried when she saw the first box of them. "Frankie, Jessica, Joey, *gatitos! Ven! Qué* cute!"

By ten to one, I'd moved twenty-two cats. You could tell a lot were gone. But there were still way too many cats walking around.

And we were out of boxes.

"You sure there are no more?" Ms. Witherspoon asked me. "Iris, did you check carefully? Maybe Will left some more for you. Maybe Sammy found some. Did you ask him? Call and ask him. Oh, Lord"—she was getting rattled—"if she sees all these cats, she'll put me out for sure! We have to do something!"

"We will!" I tried to swallow back my panic. "We'll hide them! We'll put them somewhere."

"They won't like that!"

"They don't have to like it!" Don't panic, Iris. If I panicked and she panicked . . . "We don't have to hide all of them." I tried to smile. "I mean, you're the Cat Lady, right? There have to be some cats walking around, or they'll know something's up. We'll catch the others and put them in closets."

"We already caught the ones who let themselves be caught!" She shook her head some more. "And those are the selfsame ones who like being in the closet. Now all we've got left are the hard cases, the ones—"

"Ms. Witherspoon, you got another idea?"

"I'm telling you, it's not going to work." She sighed, crouched down, and began calling: "Here kit, kit, kit! Come on, babies! *Psss, psss, psss!* That's right. Come on, come to Mama! Iris, now move slowly. If you scare one, you'll scare all of them and we'll never catch them!"

At least two ran behind the piano, one managed to squeeze itself under the stove, and I had blood running down my hand by the time I was done, but I caught at least ten of them. We shut them in the coat closet, the bedroom closet, the broom closet, the linen closet, and the cabinet under the kitchen sink.

Marrr! They didn't like it in there. *Meouwwww! Rarrrrrrr!* It may have been ten, but it sounded like a hundred.

"Oh, Lord." Ms. Witherspoon wrung her hands. "I should have known this would happen. I should have known this when we were packing up the quiet, mild-mannered ones and leaving all the troublemakers! What are they going to do to me? That manager lady's going to know we're lying. She's going to put me out!"

The phone rang.

"It's her. She's here!" Will said.

My stomach dropped.

"She's getting out of her car. Oh, man, Iris, you were right about her. She looks mean. Yo, what's that howling?"

"It's the cats!" My heart was knocking so hard, I could hardly breathe. "We've got cats in all the closets, and they're howling!"

"Oh, Lord! And the windows aren't open yet," cried Ms. Witherspoon. "We forgot the windows. Oh, sweet Jesus!"

"Will"—I shouted to be heard over Ms. Witherspoon, who had a can of air freshener in each hand and was rushing around, spraying and praying—"Will, she can't come in till we shut these cats up! Will, you hear me? I need some time!"

"I hear you!" he said. "I'll go out in the hall and block her way. I'll keep her talking. You handle the howling."

How? Ms. Witherspoon was running from closet to closet now with that jar of catnip I'd brought her, sprinkling it in, begging them to hush, and it was doing nothing.

I needed help.

I climbed out onto the fire escape. Even from out here it sounded like a hundred cats being murdered.

"Yolanda!" I ran down and banged on her window.

"*Arrrk!* Yolanda! Yolanda!" squawked Cuca.

"The manager's here," I shouted, "and all the cats are meowing! Can you stall her?"

"*Meowww!* Stall her!" yelled Cuca.

There was a gleam in Yolanda's eye when she appeared in the window. "Yeah, I'll stall her," she said. "I'll be happy to stall her. Thinks she can leave us without an elevator for two months and then has the nerve to walk in here and bully people? Don't you worry, stalling her will be my pleasure."

"*Awwwk!* Power to the people!" screamed Cuca. "Hello, good-bye, pretty bird, ding dong! Shut up! *Rrrrrrrrrrrrr!*"

"Yolanda," I said, "I need to borrow your bird."

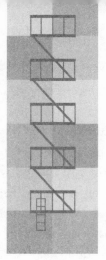

CHAPTER 23

I WASN'T SURE WHERE CUCA FIT INTO MY PLAN. I didn't have a plan. I'd barely set his cage on the kitchen table and washed the smell of cat litter off my hands when the doorbell rang.

Ms. Witherspoon bowed her head. "'The Lord is the strength of my life. Of whom shall I be afraid?'" Then we went to the living room and opened the door.

The manager was even more like Cruella De Vil than I had remembered.

"How are you today, sweetheart?" Her voice was smooth as cough medicine as she looked Ms. Witherspoon over, head to toe.

Ms. Witherspoon took my hand. "I'm fine, thank you."

"Good." The smile switched off. "I understand from Hector here"—Cruella nodded toward Mr. Ocasio, who stood on the stairs—"that you have far too many cats. I also hear"—her skinny black eyebrows went up—"that you've been flushing their waste material . . ."

Ms. Witherspoon gripped my hand tighter.

"Now we've sent you several warnings. Have you read them, dear?" She was checking out the hat. It was the good luck hat, the big black mushroom-shaped one with the bunches of cherries. I'd told Ms. Witherspoon I didn't think she should wear it. "Do you read *any* of the letters we send you, sweetheart?" I wanted to grab her bony neck and yell, Her name's Ms. Witherspoon, not Dear, not Sweetheart, sweetheart!

"Excuse me!" Yolanda puffed up the stairs, pushed past Mr. Ocasio, and planted herself between Cruella and us. "I was speaking to you, and you walked away. That's very rude." Her orange T-shirt made her look even larger than usual.

Cruella tried to put more distance between them. She switched on her smile and Mr. Rogers voice again. "I'll be happy to speak with you as soon as—"

"When we need you"—Yolanda talked right over her—"we can't get you over here for nothin'. Now, when you decide to harass a poor old woman . . . and I notice you asked how she is, but you didn't ask me about my health! I got high blood pressure. And Mrs. Serrano"—she tipped her chin toward Luisa, who had come up the stairs with Raymond and Andy—"has bad asthma. So does my son. And while you're asking, try asking Ocasio. You know how many times a day he has to run up and down these steps because you people won't fix the elevator? You know how many times we all do?"

Cruella's cell phone rang. "Whaaat?" she barked into it. "Yeah, I'm here. Yeah"—she checked her watch—"it'll only take a minute. I just have to look at this one apartment."

"You're gonna look at her apartment before you look at mine?" Yolanda seemed to swell up even larger. "I know you're new here, but five comes before six. You're supposed to do these things in order. Mrs. Serrano is a senior citizen and she has serious problems in her apartment, too—"

"*Sí!*" Luisa nodded. "*Hay un leak en la bañera, y*—"

"What's she saying?" Cruella asked Mr. Ocasio.

"You don't speak Spanish?" Yolanda said. "That's not right. You never heard of community relations? They should send somebody who knows how to talk to people."

I could have kissed Yolanda!

But Cruella was elbowing me aside to get away from her, pushing past Ms. Witherspoon into the apartment. "Put it in writing, ladies. Write me a letter. Send me a list of your complaints and I'll see they're taken care of. Excuse me! Come with me, Hector. Okay, ladies?

Write me a letter. Thank you." And she closed the door in Yolanda's face.

I held my breath as we followed her inside, but I didn't hear any howls. The catnip must have worked! The cat that always sat under the lamp was under the lamp, but I didn't see any others. And so far, I didn't smell anything!

The cell phone rang again. "Whaaat!" Cruella said. "I know. I know." She went into the bedroom, phone to her ear, Mr. Ocasio tagging behind her. We followed. "What can I tell you? They don't get it!" she said to the person on the other end. "They're going on about the elevator, like that's the cause of everybody's problems." There was a cat on top of the wardrobe. I prayed she wouldn't spot it. There was a lump under the bedspread that had to be a cat. "Yeah, I told that to the kid in 3B," she said. "I said, the elevator is not the cause. It's the result. A result that could so easily be avoided if—"

"If you put me out on the street!" Ms. Witherspoon said under her breath.

I grabbed her hand again.

"Hold on, Jason"—Cruella checked her watch again—"Hector, I don't have all day. You said this place was crawling with cats. I've seen two cats. Where are the cats?"

So she hadn't spotted them! But just as I was starting to relax, I heard scratching coming from the closet in the piano room. And then a high, shaky mew. Mr. Ocasio looked at us but didn't say anything. I could see a cat on the piano bench, but that's not who was mewing. If we were lucky, it was Cuca. If we weren't, and the catnip was wearing off . . .

Cruella walked in the piano room. I heard another mew.

Cuca was good, but he wasn't that good. I faked a coughing fit.

"It's Jitters," whispered Ms. Witherspoon. "My good luck hat isn't working! Dear Lord, please don't let Jitters get the others started! Or keep this lady talking to Jason so she doesn't notice. Iris, what's that prayer you said to me before? Something about not being timid and having purpose—"

I stopped coughing. "It wasn't from the Bible. It was from my typing book."

"I don't care where it's from," she said, "if it can give us courage! We could use some courage."

That's when I remembered the Mildred Dornbush letter.

Why had it taken me this long to think of it?

I ran back to the living room and dialed Will's number. "Will! That complaint letter we did? Is it still in your computer?"

"Yeah," he said. "What's up?"

"She said write her a letter!" I was too excited to whisper, so giddy that I wanted to dance around the room. "But she only said it 'cause she thought no one here would do it!"

"Won't she be in for a surprise," he said. "I'm going to the desk right now!"

I checked to make sure she wasn't coming. "So you can get rid of the lass's asses and fix it up and print it out?"

"I'm here!" I heard the whirr of his computer starting. "We're booting up. Oh, man! And we thought we were just fooling around! I never thought . . ." The mouse clicked. The keyboard clacked. "Yeah, here we go. Right here!" His voice crackled with excitement. "Iris, this is perfect! We wrote a great letter! I can do this in five minutes! Call when she starts to leave. I'll be in the hall waiting."

I hurried back through the apartment. Jitters had stopped mewing. There were no cats walking around. When I got to the kitchen, Cruella was off the phone and Ms. Witherspoon, her good luck hat clutched to her chest, seemed to be making a speech. From Mr. Ocasio's and Cruella's faces, it had been going on ever since I left.

"The world is full of people who need cats and kittens," she was saying. "That's right. Some of them might not know it yet, and some of them may be just finding it out, but once they come face-to-face with a cat or kitten, and have it in their house, and get to see what excellent company a kitten or cat can be . . ."

Maybe she was trying to bore Cruella into leaving. Mr. Ocasio was peering out the window like he was hoping a flying saucer would fly by and abduct him. Cruella kept checking her watch. Even Cuca had his head tucked under his wing.

Maybe it would work.

". . . giving somebody a cat is doing a good deed. The Lord put cats on this earth to bring joy and happiness where there was none . . ."

Cruella sighed loudly. "I'm not here to discuss joy and happiness. We're discussing your cats, and what to do about them."

"Miss, haven't you been listening?" Ms. Witherspoon said. "There's nothing *to* do about them. How many cats have you seen here?"

"Right now?" Cruella's lips pursed. "Three or four. But I happen to know—"

"That's right!" Ms. Witherspoon said. "Three or four. And you know why that is?" She looked at me, then raised her chin and turned back to Cruella. "It's because I've found other places for them. Yes, I have. Yes, indeed." Her voice got stronger. "We've placed them elsewhere. Isn't that true, Iris?"

"That's right." I didn't know what she was talking about. I didn't care. Will couldn't need more than two minutes.

"And you're who, again?" Cruella said, as if she had just now noticed me.

"Iris Diaz-Pinkowitz," I said. For once in my life it felt good having a name with all those syllables. "Apartment 2B." Leave, Cruella!

"Iris is assisting me," said Ms. Witherspoon. "She helps me keep my house clean, she's been helping me find good places for my babies—"

That sounded like she was considering giving the cats away. But I couldn't stop to think about it. "Anyone can have three or four cats," I said. "Three is a normal number." She did have three. Or four. Or forty-four. Time to go, Cruella. Bye-bye. See ya. *Te veo.*

But just as Cruella unfolded her arms and picked up her briefcase, a loud *mewp* came from overhead. It was Sweet William, perched on the top edge of the kitchen door.

I coughed loud as I could. Please, don't look up, Cruella! Go!

He *mewped* again.

"Shut up," I whispered.

I'd forgotten that "shut up" was Cuca's favorite word. A *brrrk* came from the cage. Then, "Shut up! Awwwk! Shut up! No, you shut up!"

"Meeoooop!" Sweet William said it louder.

Cuca meowed back. Then *"BRRRRNNNG!"* he rang.

Cruella grabbed her phone. "Whaaat!" she barked.

"Whaaat!" squawked Cuca. *"Brrnnng! WHAAAT! Meeooop!"*

"What's going on?" snapped Cruella.

"Nothing!" I said. "It's just the bird."

A meow came from under the sink, then a yowl from the broom closet, and then a mew from the piano room. Then more howls, and more. Whomp! Scratch! Thunk! *MyyyYARRRRR!* Whoever was in that broom closet was desperate to get out.

Cruella's eyes narrowed. "That's not the bird!"

"No, yeah, he imitates anything," I said. "He's good!"

Mr. Ocasio opened his mouth, then closed it again.

Ms. Witherspoon looked like the world was coming to an end.

Cruella was still looking around the room like, why don't I know what's going on? But that couldn't last. So I did what I had to do. I opened the cage. "Dirty bird!" I said. "Cuca's a dirty bird!"

"Kiss my little green ass!" he screamed, flying to the top of the refrigerator. "*Awwwk!* Ends greasy buildup! *Myowwwww!*" I ducked as he flew over me. "And it's a high fly ball to center field! *Mrrrarrr!* Operators are standing by!" Cruella swung her briefcase at him as he flapped past her head. "*Raaaaarrrr!* Step OUT of the vehicle! Partly cloudy, chance of late-day showers! *Meouwwww! RARRRRRRR! Myeww! BRRKK!* I NEED A HUG!"

"Iris! Catch him!" yelled Mr. Ocasio, covering his head with his arms as Cuca flew over him.

"*Brrrrkk! Ahhhh-leluya, alleluya, alleluya, alleluya!*"
He was aiming straight for the cherries on Ms. Witherspoon's hat.

I grabbed the hat from her and handed it to Cruella.
"Hold this!" I said.

"Tomato! *Dame un tomate! Dame un besito!*" Cuca
swooped down. Was he going to kiss Cruella on the lips?
No, he was landing on the hat!

She dropped it and ran screaming into the piano
room.

"Iris, help! Shhh! Babies, hush up, now! Shush, I'm
begging you!" Ms. Witherspoon rushed from broom
closet to cabinets.

"*Cállate*, Cuca!" Mr. Ocasio grabbed a towel, threw
it over the hat and Cuca both, picked them up, shoved
them in the cage, pulled the towel out, latched the
door, and put the towel over the cage.

"You're in big trouble now, Iris!" he told me as he
carried the cage to the window and put it out on the
fire escape. "We're all in big, big trouble." He turned
to Ms. Witherspoon, who was muttering, "'Yea, in the
shadow of thy wings I will make my refuge, until these
calamities are overpast.'"

"You better start praying for a miracle!" he said
to her. "You hear that?" He nodded toward the piano
room, where, now that Cuca had shut up and the cats
were quieting down, I could hear Cruella talking. "She's
reporting all of this to the office."

I was sure, when I heard a ring an instant later, that it was the office calling Cruella back, or Cuca *brrrnging* from the fire escape. It rang two more times before I realized it was Ms. Witherspoon's kitchen phone.

"Iris, how's it going up there? Do I have more time?" Will sounded panicked. "I've got the letter done, but what's Cruella's name? Do you even know the landlord's name? I can't give her a letter that's not addressed to anyone. She'll throw it in the garbage!"

I panicked, too. But only for a second. I'd just remembered something Mildred had said about complaint letters. "Hold on, Will. Miss?" I called into the piano room. Cuca had shut up. The cats had stopped howling. "Could you come in here?"

Cruella came over to the kitchen doorway.

"What's your name?" I said.

"Ms. Green," she said. "Why?"

"With an 'e' on the end, or without?" I said.

"No 'e.' Who are you talking to?"

"And your company's name?" I said.

"It's ABC Realty," put in Mr. Ocasio.

"Ms. Green. No 'e.' ABC Realty," I told Will. "You can address the letter to Ms. Green at ABC Realty."

"What letter? Who are you talking to?" Cruella said as Will's keyboard clacked.

My brain was whirring faster than the computer.

"Will," I said watching Cruella's face. "You're making a copy of the complaint letter for our congressman, right? And the mayor? And the governor?"

"We're complaining to the government?" Ms. Witherspoon's eyes got very wide.

"You're not complaining about me?" said Mr. Ocasio.

"No," I said. "Ms. Green said she needed a letter. So we wrote her a letter."

"Yo, Iris," Will said. "There's an Office of the Handicapped! Should we send one to them, too?"

"Yeah, you're handicapped. Definitely to the Office of the Handicapped! I'll call Eyewitness News, too! Bet we'll get on the six o'clock news. And while we're at it—"

Cruella picked up her briefcase. "Let's go, Hector! I've wasted enough time. I've got buildings to manage." She punched a number into her cell phone. "Jason, I'm out of here. This was a complete waste of my time!"

She started for the front of the apartment.

Ms. Witherspoon followed her. "I don't think it was a waste of your time at all," she said. "Not if it puts your mind to rest about my cats!"

"And not if you fix the elevator!" I called after them.

I was still holding the phone. "Iris, you there?" Will yelled. "What's going on? The letter's done."

"Okay, Ms. Green," I yelled. "You can pick up the letter on your way down the stairs! Will, don't hang up." I lowered my voice to make sure they didn't hear. "Will," I said, "you did take out the dead ducks?"

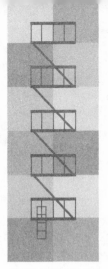

CHAPTER 24

WILL WAS RIGHT THERE ON THE THIRD FLOOR
landing when Cruella came down the stairs. "Ms.
Green!" He looked about to bubble over as he handed
her the letter. "Ms. Green, this is for you!"

"Wait a minute, Will! Hold up!" called Yolanda. I'd
rung her doorbell and Luisa's on the way down. There
were nine of us now crowding outside Will's door.
"Will, what's that you gave her?"

"Remember how Ms. Green said she needed a letter?" I said. "Well . . ."

"Here's the letter!" Will said.

"About how they have to fix the elevator now!" I
said. "So Will can get to school."

Luisa gasped. Yolanda let out a whoop. Ms. Witherspoon's eyes were shining.

"*Qué pasó?* What's happening? What's all this com-

196

motion?" Daisy ran down the stairs with her three grandkids. "I don't believe it!" she said after Luisa explained in Spanish. "And I missed all of it!"

"Yes, you did." Ms. Witherspoon straightened her hat, which she'd made Mr. Ocasio get from Cuca's cage before we left. "It's all over. Ms. Green's just fixing to leave. Now that she's walked through my house and seen my few little cats and heard how they've been placed, she's going to go away and leave us be—"

"Not before we hear this letter!" Yolanda snatched it from Cruella, who was about to stick it in her briefcase. "This is a letter I have to hear. Plus, now"—she moved in front of the stairs in case Cruella tried to escape—"if she claims she never got it, or she don't respond, we have witnesses—"

"I don't . . . I never . . . I'll respond . . ." Cruella tried to huff. But all the huff had gone out of her.

"Here, you read it," Yolanda said, handing the letter back to Will.

"Would you?" he asked me under his breath.

For a second, my throat clenched, as if this were school.

"Don't be afraid, sugar," Ms. Witherspoon whispered. "Here, you can wear this." She took off the hat, squashed from being stuffed in the birdcage, and put it on my head. "It worked for me—"

The kids snickered. I could see Daisy and Yolanda trying not to laugh. No way was I reading in front of everyone with a mushroom on my head. I took it off and cleared my throat. "'Dear Ms. Green: I live at 532 West 109th Street, Apartment 3B. The elevator has been broken for six weeks. My father has called the landlord at least once a week...'" Whoa! This was a good letter! Even Mildred would be proud. "'... There are old people in this building and babies in strollers...'"

"Amen!" said Ms. Witherspoon.

"That's the truth!" said Daisy.

"'Not to mention that I myself am in a wheelchair...'" I looked at Will to see if this was making him too embarrassed.

That's when I happened to glance over the banister and saw Mami coming up the stairs to our apartment.

My first thought was to stop reading and hide behind Yolanda. But everyone was waiting to hear this, even Yolanda's and Daisy's kids. And Cruella was looking more and more worried. "'School starts the day after tomorrow,'" I read, "'and without an elevator I don't see—'" Why was Mami home so early?

"Iris?" She dropped her grocery bags in front of our door and ran up the stairs. "Iris, what's going on?" She looked from me, holding the mushroom hat, to Ms. Witherspoon, to Mr. Ocasio, to Cruella in her high heels and fancy suit, then to Will, who she hadn't even known existed. "What are you doing up here? What are you reading?"

"A letter to the landlord," said Yolanda, making

room for her. "This lady"—she nodded toward Cruella—"is the landlord—"

"I was just leaving," said Cruella.

"Yo, not without this!" Will grabbed the letter from me and stuck it in her hand. "And don't forget, the minute you leave, we're calling Eyewitness News and sending copies to the mayor and the Office of the Handicapped, and—"

"That's not necessary!" Cruella practically knocked Mami over to get down the stairs. Mr. Ocasio ran after her. "You don't have to do that. You don't need to send it to anyone! I'll have the elevator company here first thing tomorrow."

"Yessss!" Will shook my hand.

"Thank you, Jesus!" said Ms. Witherspoon.

Yolanda did a dance.

Mami's mouth was hanging open.

I felt like a balloon about to burst. "Will and I did the complaint letter," I told her.

"No," Will said. He'd been looking from me to Mami this whole time. "We wrote it together. Iris typed it."

"You typed it on the computer?" Now Mami's mouth was really hanging open.

"That's not all they did!" Yolanda looked over the banister to make sure Cruella was gone. "If it wasn't for Iris, Ms. Green'd be putting this lady and her cats out on the street right now!"

"Are we keeping them? Can we keep the cats?"

Raymond and Andy started tugging at her. "Please, Mami, can we, pretty please? I love them. It's only four."

"Do I look like I want four cats?" said Yolanda. "And you don't even know if Ms. Witherspoon's giving them away. Iris promised me we were just storing them."

Uh-oh. Will and I looked at each other. We'd forgotten about getting the cats back upstairs. If his dad came home and found them . . . and now with Mami home . . .

"'Buela, can we keep the kittens? 'Buela, I need them! I really need them! Please, 'Buela? Pleasey, pleasey?" Daisy's grandkids joined in, too.

"Iris, look what you started!" said Daisy.

"That's right!" Ms. Witherspoon's smile had been getting bigger and bigger. "We have Iris to thank for all of this. Iris and Will—"

"I won't be saying thank you if I end up with six kittens," said Daisy.

"Everyone needs cats and kittens," said Ms. Witherspoon. "Some might not know it yet, and some may be just finding it out, but once they're face-to-face with a cat or kitten, and have it in their house . . . and I'll be doing a very good deed, spreading joy and happiness—"

"My husband can't stand cats," said Yolanda. But she was smiling, too.

"What about you, Ms. Pinkowitz?" Ms. Wither-spoon asked Mami. "Do you like cats? Because I know Iris does."

Oh, no! I'd decided it as soon as I saw Mami wasn't mad. But I didn't want Ms. Witherspoon to say it. I had to be the one who asked Mami—after she'd digested all this, after I'd figured out whether she needed to know about Just Ask Iris, after I'd decided how to tell her about the bra. I held my breath.

But before Mami could answer, Ms. Witherspoon took her hand. "Because if you do," she said, "you'll know what I'm saying when I tell you this. Ms. Pinkowitz, I thought my babies were the best thing that had ever happened to me. But that was because I hadn't met your daughter."

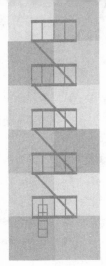

CHAPTER 25

THE ELEVATOR COMPANY GOT THERE FIRST thing the next morning. By noon, they had the elevator running. By 12:01, I was on it. Will was waiting when the doors opened on his floor. "Yo, how is it in there?" he asked.

"Great!" I said.

"Then hold the door for me! We have cats and litter to move."

We'd moved the cats out of Will's and back to Ms. Witherspoon's before his dad got home yesterday, but we'd left the cats at Daisy's, Luisa's, and Yolanda's.

The first stop was Daisy's. "*Mira*, you think you can leave some of them kittens here one more day?" she said when she let us in. I could see her trying not to look too nosy as she stared at Will's wheelchair. "I'm not saying I'm taking them. It's just"—she shrugged—

"the kids are having so much fun with them, and if they wake up from their naps and find I gave Sneaky, Squeaky, and Muñeca back . . ."

"Oh"—I tried not to grin—"I'm sure Ms. Witherspoon won't mind."

"You have to explain to her I'm not keeping them. We're just borrowing them."

"I understand," I said very seriously. But as soon as we were out the door, I clapped Will on the back. "If she named them, it's all over! We can tell Ms. Witherspoon we just placed three cats!"

Luisa took Snowball and Bo Peep.

Yolanda gave back all her cats. "But I have a girl-friend who'll probably take one," she said, "and there's another girl I could call, too, and my uncle has a store and he's always complaining about the mice, and I'll keep thinking . . ."

"So how many cats d'you have left now?" Will asked Ms. Witherspoon after we'd returned the cats who were being returned and she'd introduced Will to Sweet William, Heckle, Jekyll, Hyacinth, Chester, Peanuts, and at least a dozen others.

"I don't believe in counting," she said.

"Then, no offense," he said, "I suggest we keep the cat hotels. In case Cruella comes back."

"Oh yeah, we're keeping the cat hotels!" I said. "Don't worry."

Fluffy rubbed against my leg. I picked him up. He

pushed his nose in my neck and started purring, then reached up a paw and batted at my earring.

"Buster, behave yourself!" Ms. Witherspoon scolded him.

"It's okay," I said, nuzzling him.

"He certainly has formed a remarkable attachment to you," she said.

He was chewing on the earring now. "That's because I love him," I said.

A sad look came into her eyes. Her mouth tightened. "Well, Buster Brown," she said, "I suppose I just have to keep reminding myself that the world is full of people who need cats and kittens. Even if there are certain rascally troublemakers I hate to part with." She stroked his head, then mine. "And that I'm lucky to have Iris to make sure we find exactly the right people, and to help me keep up—"

"Iris and me," Will said. "You're forgetting about me."

It took most of the afternoon to get the cat litter off the fire escape, bagged up, and down to the cans in the basement. I carried bags. We hung garbage bags on the back of the wheelchair.

"What does this say about me that I'm having such a good time hauling Kitty Litter?" Will said when we finished. He'd unlocked his door, but I could see he wasn't ready to go in.

"Whatever it says, it says the same thing about me," I said.

"Yeah, well, we won't be doing much more of it," he said.

"Why not?" I said. "We're just getting going."

"Yeah, I know." He'd stopped looking at me. "But everyone always talks like things will stay the same. And they never do."

I didn't like the way he was looking, suddenly—like his old pinchy, peashooter face, except way sadder. "What things are we talking about?"

"I don't know. You know." He started fiddling with his keys. "Everything." He opened his door. "Tomorrow's school."

"Will, you like school, remember?" I said. "I'm the one who's worrying about it."

He still didn't look at me. "You say that now, but you'll go there, you'll make real friends, regular, normal-type friends, not just a bunch of—"

"Yeah, right." I put on an eager-beaver smile and in a goofy voice said, "Hi, I'm Iris!" then answered myself, "*So?*" in my meanest sneer. "Will," I said. "Forget school!"

But I couldn't forget school. Think about cats, I told myself all evening, or people who might want cats. Or count cats, I told myself as I lay in bed. Think about a cat-advertising flyer, or how to tell Mami we were taking Fluffy. Instead, I dug up every mean, sneering thing anyone had ever said to me, plus some no one had thought of yet. *Pinkowitz? You don't look pink to me. Did you see what that new girl's wearing? Who, the skinny one with the weird name and the big titties?* Then the teacher voices started. *And you think you belong at the Computer School why? Excuse me, what is this girl doing here? I'm sorry, dear, but somebody's made a mistake.* Around midnight, I gave up trying to sleep and started reading.

"Iris, why are you still up?" I shut the musty old brown book as soon as I heard Mami's voice, but my face must have given me away. "I thought I hid that from you!" she said as she came in. "I should have thrown that sexual surrender book in the garbage!"

"It's not the sexual surrender book," I said. "It's just something Ms. Witherspoon gave me."

I shoved *You and Your New Cat* under my pillow.

"Iris, stop worrying," she said. "Go to sleep."

I had a funny feeling, as she leaned over and I caught a whiff of Crest and almond soap and hand cream, and she smoothed my hair and kissed me, pulled up the covers, and began tucking them real tight the way she used to when I was little, that something was going to come blurting out of my mouth. I thought it might be, "Ma, I'm so nervous!" Or maybe, "Mami, we have a cat." But it wasn't. It was, "I got a bra."

"You what?" She stopped tucking. "Are you serious? How? Where'd you get it from?" Her eyes were only a few inches from mine.

My heart pounded. "I bought it."

She straightened up. "Yourself?"

I nodded.

"Where'd you get the money?"

"I earned it," I said. "Doing things for people in the building."

She shook her head. "And how long have you had this bra?"

"A week."

"A week? You went and bought yourself a bra a week ago and you didn't say anything to me?" So many looks flicked across her face, I couldn't tell if she was mad, or upset, or what she was feeling. "So you gonna show it to me?"

"You want to see it?" I jumped out of bed, trashing her neat tucking job, got the bra from my dresser, and held it out to her.

"You gonna put it on?"

I turned my back, took off my pajama top, and put it on.

"Here, let me help you." She came over and did up the hook.

I turned around.

"Well, it fits good," she said. "You picked a nice one. Where'd you get it at?"

"Over on the East Side." I still hadn't looked her in the eyes. "At this underwear store."

"You went all the way over to the East Side?"

I shrugged. "We were trying to avoid seeing anybody Freddy knew."

She let out a laugh. "You got your brother to go with you? I've heard some surprising things in the past few days, Iris, but this takes the cake!"

"He didn't go in." I told her about how he'd crossed the street when he saw Victoria's Secret, how he'd pulled his sweatshirt hood down almost to his nose, how he'd lurked outside the store.

"*Ay, Dios mío!* I can just picture it!" She laughed full out, but she had tears in her eyes. "I'm happy you have a big brother to take you, but *m'ija*"—she shook her head—"that should of been me who went with you. Yeah"—she hugged me so hard, I could hardly breathe—"that was supposed to be me."

"It's okay, Ma," I said into her shoulder. "It worked out."

"I guess it did." She stopped hugging me and started messing with my bra straps, pulling one up higher on my shoulder, loosening one little clasp thing, tightening the other. When she finished with the straps, she started straightening the elastic. Then she stepped back and looked at me, looking me over, almost like I was some strange girl she'd never seen before. It would have been embarrassing, except for the shine in her eye. "So Iris," she said. "You went to work so you could buy yourself a bra. You typed that letter to the landlord. You got anything else to add to that list of surprises?"

Should I tell her about Fluffy now? "Not yet."

"Because I'm starting to think maybe I don't need to be all that worried about you surrendering," she said. "You're not the surrendering type, are you?"

"Nope," I said.

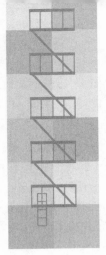

CHAPTER 26

YOU'D THINK AFTER THAT I'D HAVE FELT READY for anything, but it wasn't so easy. By the time Will rang the bell the next morning I'd changed my clothes twice, braided and unbraided my hair three times, and checked myself in the mirror a thousand times— in between begging Freddy to hurry up in the bathroom, trying to talk him into walking Blackie, walking Blackie, choking down breakfast, and going over my travel route and schedule with Mami till I was ready to explode.

Will looked very together with his ironed shirt, and his hair still wet and neatly combed, and his messenger bag slung over the back of his wheelchair. But he seemed even more uptight than I was.

We didn't talk at all going down in the elevator. "So my dad went to work," he said as he bumped himself down the three steps to the sidewalk. "I told him I'd be fine."

"Oh, yeah?" I wondered how he was going to get back up the steps after school, but I knew better than to ask. I followed him over to the curb. "What time does your bus come?"

We peered down the street. Nothing. I had to pee. Should I run back upstairs or wait for school? The girl's room—that was too scary to think about.

"What time does the bus come?" I said again.

"I just told you," he said. "Seven thirty-five."

"Oh, right." He had. Was there such a thing as tongue exercises? I never knew tongues got so tense. "Last night, when I was trying to go to sleep?" I said. "I tried counting up the cats. I got to twenty-nine names. That's not including Fluffy and the ones we gave away. D'you think we'll ever know how many cats—"

He checked his watch. I checked my watch. It was almost time for me to leave.

"D'you ever hear of a cat fair?" I said. "Where you'd have, like, a bunch of cats out on the street so people can adopt them? I mean, since Ms. Wither-spoon seems to be into giving cats away, I was thinking sometime maybe we could make signs with the cats' names on them, and tape the signs to the cat hotels, and then bring them all down here, or over to Broadway with her wagon. I mean, I don't know if she'd let us . . ."

Every time a car came down the street, he craned forward. There were lots of cars. Also cabs, vans, delivery trucks. Just no buses.

". . . the problem is, we'd have to tape the boxes shut so they couldn't jump out, and then people couldn't see them. Though that might be a plus, for the ugly ones. And then we'd have to, like, make up advertising flyers, and I was trying all night to come up with a name and a slogan, but the only things I came up with were, like, 'Loneliness up the wazoo? Something missing in your life? Do you need a cat and you don't know it? Call We Place Cats Unlimited,' which sucks, or Mildredy things like, 'Will: The lad is Gladd. Iris: The lass has class,' which is even worse—"

He wasn't listening. But if I stopped talking, my tongue might freeze up totally, and then when I got to school and they wanted to know why I was late . . .

"Iris," Will said. "You don't have to stand here and entertain me."

Entertain him? Is that what he called this?

He looked down the street for the millionth time. "Iris, don't you have to leave?"

I was scared to check my watch again. "But if I leave, you'll be alone." I'd be alone. I couldn't think about that. "What'll you do if it doesn't come? D'you have the phone? Can you call your dad?"

"No. I told him I'll be fine," he said. "I told him I'd work it out."

This wasn't good. If he was scared, and I was scared . . .

But there must be a patron saint of buses, because at that very moment, a small orange bus turned onto our block.

"Will!" I grabbed his arm. "Will, is that it?"

"That's it." He cleared his throat. He sat up straighter. "Listen, Iris, if you need to leave now . . ."

The bus pulled up in front of us. The driver walked back and slid open the side door. "Will, my man! My first pickup of the day. Whassup?" He pressed a button, and with a whirring, grinding noise, a metal platform thing began to lower. He looked at my face, at my hand still clutching onto Will's arm. "Hmmmm"—he gave Will a huge grin—"I see somebody's been having a good summer. The man's got himself a friend."

That had to embarrass Will. I let go of his arm like it was electrified.

The platform thing was even with the sidewalk now. Will backed up, turned the chair around, and backed onto it. But when I saw his face again, he didn't look embarrassed. In fact, he looked like somebody trying hard not to smile.

"The first part of the summer wasn't too great," he told the driver, "but—"

"Sorry I was late," the driver said. "Traffic. You know how it is."

"No problem." Will eased the chair into position on

the platform and bent over to lock the wheels. "I knew you'd be here. I told my dad you'd be here. I told him I'd be fine." He looked up at me. "Because I knew my friend would wait with me."

He was flat out smiling now. "Yeah, the beginning of the summer sucked," he told the driver. "But the end was really good. Yo, beam me up, Scotty! We don't want Iris to be late for school."

His smile got bigger and bigger as the platform began to rise, till it was this, like, crazy grin.

So why then, when he unlocked the wheels and began backing into the bus, did I feel like I was going to cry?

"Iris?" He stopped moving. "You better hurry up and get to school and get it over with so you can get back home. If we're doing this cat fair thing, we better do it. Before Ms. Witherspoon changes her mind about giving the cats away—"

I felt my throat loosening, my tongue beginning to unfreeze. "You think it's a good idea?"

"Yeah," he said, "but I don't like We Place Cats Unlimited. If we're gonna change the name, how 'bout Just Ask Iris and Will?"

"Or Iris and Will Unlimited," I said.

"That works," he said.

It definitely worked. I took a deep breath. I hitched up my bra strap. "I'll see you after school?"